THE SHIP of LOST SOULS

THE HUNT for the PANTHER

Accelerated Reader
Interest Level: MG
Grade/Book Level: 4.3

THE SHIP of LOST SOULS

THE HUNT for the PANTHER

by Rachelle Delaney

Grosset & Dunlap
An Imprint of Penguin Group (USA) Inc.

GROSSET & DUNLAP
Published by the Penguin Group
Penguin Group (USA) Inc., 375 Hudson Street, New York, New York 10014, USA
Penguin Group (Canada), 90 Eglinton Avenue East, Suite 700, Toronto,
Ontario M4P 2Y3, Canada (a division of Pearson Penguin Canada Inc.)
Penguin Books Ltd, 80 Strand, London WC2R 0RL, England
Penguin Ireland, 25 St Stephen's Green, Dublin 2, Ireland
(a division of Penguin Books Ltd)
Penguin Group (Australia), 707 Collins Street, Melbourne, Victoria 3008, Australia
(a division of Pearson Australia Group Pty Ltd)
Penguin Books India Pvt Ltd, 11 Community Centre,
Panchsheel Park, New Delhi—110 017, India
Penguin Group (NZ), 67 Apollo Drive, Rosedale, Auckland 0632, New Zealand
(a division of Pearson New Zealand Ltd)
Penguin Books, Rosebank Office Park, 181 Jan Smuts Avenue,
Parktown North 2193, South Africa
Penguin China, B7 Jaiming Center, 27 East Third Ring Road North,
Chaoyang District, Beijing 100020, China

Penguin Books Ltd, Registered Offices: 80 Strand, London WC2R 0RL, England

Text copyright © 2013 by Rachelle Delaney. Illustrations copyright © 2013 by
Penguin Group (USA) Inc. Map copyright © 2013 Fiona Pook. All rights reserved.
Published by Grosset & Dunlap, a division of Penguin Young Readers Group,
345 Hudson Street, New York, New York 10014. GROSSET & DUNLAP
is a trademark of Penguin Group (USA) Inc. Printed in the U.S.A.

Library of Congress Cataloging-in-Publication Data is available.

ISBN 978-0-448-45781-9 (pbk)   10 9 8 7 6 5 4 3 2 1
ISBN 978-0-448-45780-2 (hc)   10 9 8 7 6 5 4 3 2 1

ALWAYS LEARNING   **PEARSON**

For the Inkslingers

CHAPTER ONE

"Water?"

"Check."

"Map?"

"Check."

"Empty pockets for filling with plunder?"

Jem Fitzgerald pulled his pockets inside out to show how empty they were. "Check. We're ready, Captain." He tucked his pockets back in his trousers. "We should get going."

Scarlet McCray bit her lip. "Right . . . It's just . . ." She looked up at the afternoon sky and watched a flock of green parrots flap by overhead. "I have a feeling I'm forgetting something."

Jem sighed. The captain of the Lost Souls, he knew, was not forgetting anything. She just didn't want to leave her beloved Island X. "Look, it's only for a day—" he began.

"Don't rush me, Fitz," Scarlet snapped. "I just *know* I'm forgetting something."

Jem rolled his eyes. "Okay, okay," he muttered. "Take your time, then."

"I will, thanks," she retorted, crouching to retie her bootlaces.

"Fine." Jem folded his arms over his chest.

"Fine," Scarlet said to her boot.

Jem took a deep breath and counted to ten. They'd left Island X only a few times since arriving there two months before. But each time they did, Scarlet would stall until the last possible moment. He always tried to hurry her up, but there was only so much prodding the captain of the Lost Souls would take. She'd already threatened to string Tim Sanders up by his toes for calling her a slowpoke. Even when she was nowhere near her ship, Scarlet couldn't help but act like a pirate.

Jem turned away and surveyed the lush green clearing around them, which was slowly beginning to feel like home. Well, as much as a tropical island inhabited by smelly wild pigs, mischievous monkeys, and the odd poisonous tree *could* feel like home.

He shaded his eyes from the sun and squinted at the small but sturdy tree houses perched on the clearing's edge. The sight of them made him stand up a little taller. As Head of the Housing Committee, he had directed the entire building project, bringing a touch of civilization to the wilds of Island X. Of course, it was nothing like his real home, back in the Old World. Here lanterns were lit by fireflies rather than flame, and everyone slept in hammocks instead of real beds. And though it was nice to hear the rain patter on their leafy rooftops at night, sturdy wooden beams would have been much more effective in keeping out curious, hungry animals. Every now and then, Jem would wake, certain he'd heard something other than birds and bugs in the trees around them. Something *big*. Something with *claws*. Something—

Scarlet let out a loud grunt, and Jem glanced down. She was untieing and retieing her bootlaces as if her life depended on the loops being perfectly even. He shook his head and turned back to the houses. Yes, real doors would be nice. And shutters for the windows. But these would have to wait until he returned from their trip to Port Aberhard. For whether Scarlet liked it or not, she'd been summoned to the nearby port by the only person in the world she actually had to answer to—her father.

"Blast! Blimey and bilge!" Scarlet swore as her bootlace snapped in two. "Stupid boots. Why do I have to wear them at all? They're such a waste of—" She looked up at Jem. "What?"

"What, what? I didn't say anything." He took a step back, not liking the glint in her eyes. Mad Captain McCray, as the crew sometimes called her, had a glare that made even the fiercest pirate's knees quake.

"You're giving me that look," she said, eyes narrowing.

"What look? I wasn't giving you any look," Jem protested.

"You were. It was a 'buck up, McCray, going into port's not so bad' kind of look."

"It was not," said Jem, although he suspected that was exactly the look he'd been giving her. Going into port wasn't really *that* bad.

She glared at him a moment longer, then looked down at her bootlaces and sighed. When she glanced back up, the angry look had been replaced by a downright mournful one. "I just hate to leave the island," she muttered.

Jem sighed. Part of him wanted to point out that they should have been halfway to port by now. But two months under Scarlet's command had taught him that wasn't the way to get things done. He swallowed his impatience and knelt down beside her.

"Look, I know these father-daughter meetings are a pain, but look on the bright side."

Scarlet raised an eyebrow.

"Well . . ." Jem swallowed, thinking hard. "You get to catch up on all the port news."

Scarlet looked unconvinced.

He tried again. "We can steal some of those preserves you like."

Scarlet shrugged.

Jem decided to change tactics. "It's only for one night. We'll be back tomorrow afternoon, and everything will be fine. Nothing will have changed."

Two small black monkeys scampered by, shrieking.

"For instance," he continued, "the monkeys will still be up to no good."

"Come back here!" A ginger-haired girl raced by in hot pursuit. Two purple butterflies clung to her braids, and a small chameleon poked its head out of her shirt pocket.

"And Ronagh will still be working on her menagerie," he added. Scarlet nodded and managed a tiny smile.

"And doubtless, Smitty will still be head over heels in love." He batted his eyes at Scarlet. Finally, she laughed.

"Did I hear my name?" A tall, blond boy appeared behind them.

Jem grinned at Scarlet. "I didn't mention Horace. Did you?"

Scarlet giggled. "You mean Walter? Nope."

After several years as a Lost Soul, Smitty still refused to tell the crew his real name—"Smitty" came from "Smith," his last name. So they continued to call him by the worst names they could think of, assuming that one day they'd guess correctly.

"We ready to go yet?" asked Smitty.

"Yes," Jem answered, just as Scarlet said, "Not quite."

Jem's shoulders sagged.

"That's fine," said Smitty. "I'll just go say good-bye to Sina one last time." He turned and trotted off across the clearing.

Jem looked Scarlet squarely in the eye. "Okay, Captain," he said. "If you won't do it for yourself, then do it for Sina. We need to get Smitty off this island before he drives her completely mad."

Scarlet considered this. "I heard he showed up at her tree house this morning and insisted on serving her breakfast. And singing all the way through."

Jem nodded. "Exactly."

Scarlet held up her hands in defeat. "All right, Fitz. You win. We'll go."

He scrambled to his feet and pulled her up before she could change her mind. But she'd only taken a few steps toward the tree houses when she stopped and raised a hand to her forehead.

"Oh no," Jem groaned under his breath. He'd been so close.

"Shh." Scarlet closed her eyes for a moment. When she opened them, she announced, "It's the aras."

"Of course it is." Jem sighed.

"They need me," said Scarlet.

"Right."

"It could be important. I'll be right back. You go and gather the crew, and I'll meet you by the tree houses. I *will*," she added when he raised an eyebrow. "Promise."

He watched her jog off across the clearing and cursed Scarlet's favorite birds. It was entirely possible—probable, even—that they hadn't called for her at all, and she was just making one last effort to stall. But unlike Scarlet, Jem didn't have the ability to channel the island's wildlife and know when they were in distress, upset with each other, or even just hungry. So he couldn't say for sure.

And anyway, the aras *were* important. Hunted to near extinction by pirates and King's Men for their beautiful red feathers, the birds were a treasure beyond everyone's expectations. They actually collected rubies, digging them out of the ground with their beaks and tucking them by the dozens inside their nests. The Lost Souls had made it their mission to protect the birds, the jewels, and the entire island from all the treasure-hungry pirates and King's Men in the tropics.

"Is she *still* stalling?" Tim asked, appearing at Jem's side. He pushed his spectacles up on his nose. "This is crazy!"

"She says the aras need her now," Jem said, and Tim snorted. "I know," Jem agreed. "But I think she's almost ready this time."

"That's what you said two hours ago," Tim said. He took off his spectacles, wiped them on his shirt, then perched them on his nose again. "Can't you hurry her up?"

Jem gave him a withering look and began to walk toward the tree houses. The quartermaster always got twitchy when he'd been away from their ship, the *Margaret's Hop*, for too long. "You go find Emmett and Edwin," he called over his shoulder. "I'll grab Smitty and Liam, and we'll head off as soon as she gets back."

"Good luck with that," Tim yelled back. "Last I heard, Smitty was reciting love poems for Sina. It might take even longer to drag him away than the captain."

Jem groaned again. Getting the small crew of Lost Souls off Island X for a quick trip to port was hard enough with a reluctant captain. A lovesick crewmate he could do without.

He found Smitty standing by himself near his tree house, watching a crowd of Lost Souls play Monkey in the Middle nearby.

"Isn't she beautiful, Fitz?" Smitty said without taking his eyes off the crew.

Jem didn't have to ask whom he was talking about. Smitty had been hopelessly in love with Sina since they'd first met her a few weeks before. Sina and her little brother, Kapu, were native Islanders—possibly the only two who had survived the Island Fever the King's Men brought with them when they invaded the tropics.

"If only we could understand each other." Smitty sighed. "I've tried to talk to her like Scarlet does, with

7

my eyes." He gave Jem an intense stare to demonstrate. "But it doesn't seem to be working."

Jem stifled a laugh. Smitty's stare was more likely to stop a smelly wild pig in its tracks than express his affections. "Well, you're not half Islander like Scarlet is. Those two have a special connection." He couldn't quite understand it himself, but when Scarlet couldn't recall the right Islander words, and Sina couldn't understand the English ones, the two friends could read each other's thoughts.

"All right, Smit. Are you ready to go?" Jem asked. But Smitty ignored him, staring at Sina until she finally turned to look his way. He waved, but the tall, dark-haired girl rolled her eyes and turned back to the game.

"Smit!" Jem snapped his fingers in front of the boy's face.

Smitty looked at Jem. "Actually, I was thinking I might sit this trip out," he said. "Maybe I'll stay here and . . . you know." He gazed dreamily at Sina again.

"Not a chance," Jem said flatly. "You're coming to port."

"But—"

"No buts." A little bit of Scarlet seemed to have rubbed off on him. "You love a good port raid. You're coming."

Smitty shoved his hands in his pockets. "Well, that's true. And I suppose you can't very well go without me, since I *am* the best pickpocket in all the tropics."

"And so modest," Jem commented. But he was heartened to hear the smart-mouthed pirate sounding a little more like his old self. Apparently love did strange things to a person.

"Jem!" someone called, and he turned to see Gil Jenkins standing near the pool in the clearing and waving both arms. "Come quick!"

"Oh, what now?" Jem muttered, jogging off. But as soon as he saw what Gil was pointing at, he began to sprint.

Two men were stumbling across the clearing, their clothes torn and filthy. "Uncle Finn!" Jem yelled. "Thomas! What happened?"

He hadn't seen his uncle Finn or his uncle's research assistant since they'd set off to collect plant samples a few days before. They looked like they'd been wrestling crocodiles rather than searching for the rare plant that Uncle Finn believed could cure baldness.

"Jem," Uncle Finn gasped, practically collapsing into his arms. Jem staggered under his uncle's substantial weight. "Water."

"Here." Liam Flannigan tossed the explorers each a canteen, which they proceeded to gulp down without even stopping to breathe.

"What the flotsam is going on?" Scarlet appeared at Jem's shoulder, also out of breath.

"Not sure." Jem waited for Uncle Finn to catch his breath and quench his thirst so he could start explaining. Several other Lost Souls ran over to see what the commotion was all about.

Finally, Uncle Finn handed Liam the empty canteen. He wiped his mouth with his dirty sleeve and turned to Jem. Then he drew a deep breath. "Brace yourself, nephew," he said. "Of all the tales I've lived to tell, this one is by far the most terrifying."

A few Lost Souls gasped.

"What happened?" Jem whispered. Uncle Finn was famous for his dramatic storytelling, but this sounded dire, even for him.

"We met . . ." Uncle Finn paused. "The panther."

The Lost Souls gasped again.

"The panther?" Smitty repeated. "There's a panther on Island X?" He moved closer to Sina, putting a protective arm around her shoulders, which she quickly shrugged off. She pulled an arrow out of her bag and examined the sharpness of its point. Sina had the best aim on the island. Smitty tucked his arms behind his back and moved a few feet away.

"There is indeed." Uncle Finn sniffed. "If you'd studied my map, you'd have seen it."

"That's right!" Jem reached into his back pocket and whipped out the map. It wasn't Uncle Finn's original map, which the explorer had drawn decades ago while first exploring the islands, but a close reproduction that Jem had made himself. Jem shivered. "What happened?"

Uncle Finn dropped his voice to resume his dramatic tone. "We were out looking for more samples of the bromeliad that cures androgenetic alopecia," he began.

"Cures what?" Ronagh piped up.

"Baldness, remember?" Scarlet told her, pointing to Uncle Finn's head of thick, curly hair. Until recently, he'd been completely bald, proving that the bromeliad really did work miracles.

Uncle Finn smoothed down his hair. "We'd hiked farther west than we'd ever gone before when we got caught in a downpour yesterday evening. And then—"

"We found this hole in the side of a mountain," Thomas cut in. "Like a cave or a den. And it looked right warm and dry—"

"So we ventured in," Uncle Finn cut him off, shooting Thomas an irritated look. The old explorer preferred to tell his own tales. "Only to find ourselves face-to-face with . . ." He paused once more. "The biggest, snarliest, hungriest black panther we'd ever seen."

Several Lost Souls shrieked. A few more ducked behind some larger ones.

"Had you ever seen a smaller, less snarly, not-so-hungry one?" Ronagh asked.

"Quiet, Ronagh," said her brother, Liam.

"Just wondering," she muttered to the chameleon in her pocket. "Maybe there are friendlier ones."

Scarlet shook her head at the younger girl. "Don't even *think* about trying to make friends with it."

"Not on your life." Uncle Finn gave Ronagh a stern look. "We were lucky to escape with ours. And I was lucky that Thomas has the strength of ten men and could injure the beast while I made my getaway."

"You did *what*?" Ronagh cried, turning to Thomas.

"Just poked 'im in the eye, real quick," Thomas said, taking a step back from the red-faced girl. "He ain't hurt, I swear!"

"But he's angry," said Uncle Finn, his eyes gleaming. "So if you value your young lives, watch out for this beast. He lives up the western arm, but who knows where he might turn up."

Jem wiped a stream of sweat off his temple, remembering the noises he'd heard the previous night, when everyone was asleep. Port Aberhard, with its Old World streets and buildings with doors that shut and locked, was looking better by the second.

Scarlet, however, seemed to be thinking just the opposite. "Maybe . . . maybe we shouldn't go to port today," she whispered to Jem. "Maybe we're needed here."

Jem shook his head, trying to clear it of the panther and focus on their mission. "Captain, it's already late afternoon. Your father's expecting you tonight."

"But what about the crew? We can't leave them now."

"If we leave now, we'll be back tomorrow afternoon. If we stay, we'll just have to go tomorrow. You know that," he insisted. Admiral McCray had made it clear on their last visit—when they'd arrived two days late because a war broke out between two troops of monkeys—that he expected his daughter to abide by their agreement. Once every two weeks, Scarlet had to meet him in port. If she kept up her end of the bargain, he'd let her live with the Lost Souls on Island X and keep the King's Men away from it.

Sina slipped over and took Scarlet's arm. For a moment, they just looked at each other, and if Jem hadn't known about their strange method of communication, he would have assumed they were having a serious staring contest.

Finally, Scarlet grunted. "All right. Fine. I trust you," she said. Turning to Jem, she explained, "Sina will take care of things here until tomorrow. But we've got to go *now*, so we can be back as soon as possible."

Jem let out a sigh of relief. "I'm ready. We're all ready." He tossed Sina a grateful look and turned to the small crew of travelers. "Let's get going."

CHAPTER TWO

By the time they reached the *Margaret's Hop*, the sun was close to setting. Scarlet climbed aboard, followed by Tim, Jem, Smitty, Liam, and the twins, Emmett and Edwin.

Though she'd been on board a few times in the past two months, it still felt strange to be standing on deck under the mast rather than in the jungle under a tree canopy so thick it blocked out the sun. After all the years she'd spent away from Island X, she was finally beginning to feel like she belonged there again. She knew every tree on the edge of the clearing and every monkey that inhabited them— not to mention every monkey's problems, thanks to this newfound ability of hers to channel their thoughts.

Her first language was slow in returning, but Sina was a dedicated teacher. Every morning, she made Scarlet memorize a dozen words and forced her to use each one at least twice throughout the day.

Blimey, thought Scarlet, *I'm going to miss tomorrow's lesson. I should have asked Sina for some words to practice by myself. Now I'll be behind, and I'll—*

"We'll be back tomorrow afternoon," Jem reminded her, appearing at her side. "And nothing will have changed."

She shook herself back to the present. "Right. Yes. I know."

Jem handed her some nuts he'd brought along. "If you don't mind my saying, Captain," he said, "sometimes it's best to stop thinking and just . . . do."

Scarlet gulped down her nuts. He was right, as usual. She had a mission to complete. It was time to act like a captain.

She looked around. "Emmett and Edwin, weigh anchor!" she yelled at the twins. "Tim, take the wheel, and Smit, mind the mast. Liam, this deck looks like bilge—swab it quick, will you? And Fitz." She turned to him. "Check the ropes for frays and replace the worst ones."

Jem nodded and saluted. "Yes, Captain!" He set off to check the ropes.

Good old Fitz, she thought, watching the boy march off in his surprisingly clean trousers and boots. *What would I do without him?*

Soon they were out in the open ocean, sailing east toward Port Aberhard, away from the setting sun. Scarlet took a deep breath of cool, salty air, then another. Life on board the *Hop* wasn't so bad. In fact, it had been a jolly home for two years, just when she'd needed it most. She owed all she knew about being a pirate to this old boat and its crew.

She ran her hand along the weathered railing, suddenly ashamed at having neglected the *Hop*. Tim was constantly pointing out new holes in her sides and rips in her mast. "Thank you," she whispered, giving it a pat.

She walked across the main deck and up to the fo'c'sle, leaning over the edge to watch a pair of glowing

15

purple jellyfish bobbing in the water below. Then she dug around in her pocket for Uncle Finn's old spyglass and pressed it to her eye, scanning the horizon for approaching ships.

"See anything?" Tim yelled from the ship's wheel, where he studied a map and compass.

"Not a speck, Swig," Scarlet called back. Tim's love of nautical books and maps had earned him the nickname "Drivelswigger," or "Swig" for short. "Too bad—it would have been a nice night for a ship raid."

"Doubt we'll be able to get away with raiding anymore, Cap'n," Tim replied, and Scarlet lowered the spyglass. She'd forgotten, but Tim was right.

The legend of the Ship of Lost Souls had begun some ten years before, when a ship had set out carrying a class of geography students and schoolmasters from a port school. They'd gotten themselves lost in a hurricane, and the grown-ups had been tossed overboard, leaving the children to captain the ship themselves. When they finally found their way home, they learned that not only had they been presumed dead, but sailors who spotted their ship believed it to be haunted by ghosts. They called it the Ship of Lost Souls.

Instead of setting them straight, the children decided to play along, dressing up like ghouls in long black cloaks and swooping down on the ships of pirates and King's Men when they needed food or supplies. The ship soon became a magnet for children orphaned in the tropics or running away from boarding schools or ships, or in Scarlet's case, home.

"The legend had a good run," said Edwin, joining her and Tim at the wheel.

"Suppose it had to die sooner or later." Emmett sighed, appearing at her other side.

Scarlet grunted. "It'd still be alive and well if it weren't for that dog Lucas Lawrence, leaving to join a 'real' pirate ship." She still couldn't help but sneer whenever she thought of her former crew member.

"He's a bilge rat," said Emmett.

"A scurvy swine," Tim spat.

Scarlet nodded. It was the only way to describe someone who'd not only defected from the Lost Souls but told his new crew the Lost Souls' secret. Now everyone knew that they were just children. Brave and strong and clever children, of course, but children nonetheless.

"Wonder what old Lucas is up to now," said Edwin.

"No good," Scarlet answered with complete certainty. Lucas had taken off with Uncle Finn's map, so he knew exactly where the treasure was. He had convinced his new crew on the *Dark Ranger* to try to steal it once, and it was just a matter of time before they tried again. "Can we hurry?" she asked Tim.

He frowned at her over his spectacles.

"Sorry," she muttered. Sometimes a good captain had to know when to leave her quartermaster to do his job.

She picked up the spyglass again and forced herself to not look back at Island X. Instead she looked forward, at their destination, where she'd soon be meeting her father. These father-daughter meetings truly scuttled, but she'd take Jem's advice and stop fretting about them. She'd just answer her father's questions and assure him that all was well on Island X. Then she'd be back on board the *Hop* and sailing home in no time.

She reached out and tapped the wooden railing for good luck. Just in case.

"Smit, quit splashing me," Liam complained.

"Splashing? Who's splashing?" Smitty said innocently. After dropping anchor in the bay near Port Aberhard, they had all piled into their dinghy to row ashore. Smitty had insisted he take the oars.

"Argh! He did it again! Scarlet!"

"Shh, quiet, Liam," Scarlet whispered. The last thing they needed was the attention of some pirates or King's Men. "One more time, Leander, and I'm tossing you overboard," she warned Smitty.

"Then who would row us to port?" said Smitty. Despite the darkness, Scarlet could tell he was grinning.

"Me," Edwin volunteered.

"I'd do it," said Tim.

"Or me," Jem offered.

"Oh, so I'm that replaceable, am I?" Smitty *tsk*ed. "Fine then, I'll just—"

"Argh! Again!" Liam cried as Smitty's oar flicked seawater up into his face. "That's it! I'm gonna pound you!"

"Liam, sit down, you're rocking the boat!" Scarlet commanded.

"Hey!" a voice shouted from nearby. The crew froze,

then slowly looked to the right, where a grizzled old sailor stood in a rowboat, holding up a lantern. "What's goin' on there? Who are ye?"

"Tim!" Scarlet hissed, for she couldn't very well answer herself.

"Just some cabin boys, sir," Tim called back. "Heading into port for the night."

"Well, get on with ye," the sailor told them. "'Cause I sure ain't gonna rescue ye when ye end up in the drink."

"Yes, sir!" Tim called.

Scarlet kicked Smitty. "Row!"

"Bilge rat," Liam added under his breath, but Smitty pretended he hadn't heard and whistled a quiet tune.

They made it to the docks without capsizing and scrambled out of the boat, which Tim tied to a post. Already Scarlet could hear the raucous sounds of port: shouts and hollers from some drunken pirates, tinny piano music from a nearby tavern, and the crunch of heavy boots on gravel. She tried not to think about the insect orchestra that played all through the night on Island X, lulling everyone to sleep.

"Come on, crew," she said once they were all up on the dock. "Let's get this over with."

The only good thing about being in port was that children were rarely noticed. The pirates were too busy insulting and spitting at each other, and the King's Men were too busy trying to look important and keep their blue uniforms spotless. Which made it nice and easy for the Lost Souls to nab what they needed and disappear before anyone saw them.

"All right." Scarlet motioned for the crew to duck into an alley, where they huddled in the shadows. "We need some food—Edwin and Emmett, I'll leave that to you. Jem, get whatever supplies you need to finish the houses. Tim and Liam, you're on weapons—Charlie and Gil need new daggers. Oh, and some shirts and trousers. Smit, that'll be your—" She stopped when she caught sight of Smitty's face. The boy was chewing on his lower lip. "What now?" she growled.

Smitty sighed. "Well, if you must know, I just saw this piece of rope that reminded me of the way Sina braids her hair some days, and I—"

"Smitty!" Tim threw his hands in the air. "We're on a port raid! We've got things to plunder, pockets to pick! This is no time to be a swoony sea dog!"

"Wait, I know," Jem spoke up. "Smit, why don't you find a gift for Sina? You know, something nice. While you're stealing other stuff, that is."

Smitty perked up immediately. "That's a jolly idea, Fitz. Maybe I'll get her something for her hair. One of those . . . clip thingies."

Scarlet opened her mouth to point out that a gift he'd actually paid for might be more thoughtful, then shook her head. There was no time to argue. "Right. Good luck with that," she said. "Let's meet back at the dock in a few hours."

She put her fist in the middle of their huddle, and the others, who knew the tradition well, piled theirs on top of it. "No prey, no pay, mateys."

"No prey, no pay!" they echoed.

"May you die peacefully on Island X rather than have your hands chopped off by the merchant you stole from."

"Die peacefully!"

"Now get going," said Scarlet. "I've got an admiral to meet."

Scarlet made sure all her hair was tucked inside her cap and pulled it down over her eyes before slipping out of the alley. This way, if one of the King's Men spotted her father during their meeting, he'd assume the admiral was talking to some scruffy cabin boy, and not his long-lost daughter.

She headed down Port Aberhard's main road, past a tavern packed with rum-soaked pirates singing off-key chanteys. She passed an apothecary's shop boarded up for the night and sidestepped a pack of rats squealing over scraps outside the door. She could smell the jungle nearby, but its lush scent was overpowered by port smells like sour rum, horse manure, and rotting wood.

If there was one place in the tropics that did not and would never feel like home, it was Port Aberhard. Or any port town, for that matter. Not even Jamestown, where she'd lived for five years, felt remotely like home.

Her father had taken her to Jamestown after the Island Fever swept through their village when she was five years old. Scarlet's mother had begged her father to take Scarlet off the island and keep her safe from the disease that was taking many Islander lives—including, eventually, her mother's. They'd settled in a rickety old boardinghouse, and John McCray had gone back to work for the King's Men, leaving Scarlet to learn Old World ways from the world's creepiest governess, whom she called Scary Mary. After five years of English lessons, petticoats, and boots that pinched her toes until she was certain they'd fall off, she decided she'd had enough and ran away to join the Lost Souls.

Even now, port towns made Scarlet's skin crawl. It wasn't just the memories of Scary Mary forcing her to forget her past as an Islander that haunted her. It was more than that. The longer she lived on Island X, the more she felt the island's pain at being torn down and taken apart by the Old Worlders. And nowhere was that more pronounced than in port.

Don't think about it now, Scarlet told herself. *Get to your meeting, then get home to the crew.*

Dodging a pair of pirates stumbling toward her, she continued on, looking for the tiny clapboard house her father had described.

Admiral McCray insisted on holding each of their meetings in a secret location—someplace the other King's Men would never think to look for him. Last time they'd met in the cellar of a tavern, which was freezing cold and crawling with spiders. This time, however, he'd chosen someplace he insisted would be better: Voodoo Miranda's house.

It stood near the end of the street, squeezed between two brick buildings that looked like they might crumble if you shoved them hard enough. Scarlet paused out front. Every window was dark, but that didn't mean the voodoo queen wasn't home. She was probably cooking up some potion that would turn an unsuspecting person into a two-headed lizard.

Stop thinking, Scarlet told herself again. *Just do.* She gathered all the courage she could find, stepped up to the rotting door, and knocked twice.

Even though she'd seen Voodoo Miranda several times over the years, she still jumped when the front door swung open and the woman peered out, baring her crooked teeth. Easily six feet tall, Voodoo Miranda wore a long green dress that glimmered in the light of the twisted black candle she held. She had long, matted black hair that hung down to her waist, and her lips were painted a deep purple.

But that wasn't the worst of it. Coiled around her left wrist, like a big poisonous bracelet, was a shiny green python. Another snake, this one a striped viper, was nestled in her enormous hair, watching Scarlet closely.

Scarlet took a hasty step back, wiping her sweaty palms on her trousers. She hated snakes, especially the small ones that looked harmless but could kill you with one bite. "Um. Hello."

Voodoo Miranda squinted at her for a moment. Then her mouth spread into a wide purple smile. "Come in."

She stepped aside, and Scarlet darted past into a room full of dusty furniture that probably hadn't been used for years. There were black candles everywhere, and the loose floorboards creaked underfoot. Scarlet couldn't help but wonder if Voodoo Miranda hid something underneath them. Or someone . . .

Stop! she told herself. "Um, where am I meeting him?"

"In the kitchen," said Miranda. "This way." She led Scarlet down a pitch-dark hallway into another room—this one lit by a single lantern. The kitchen was cluttered with bottles and jars of every size and color, and it smelled like long-dead flowers that needed to be tossed out. A small cloudy window looked out onto a dark yard.

"Don't mind my work," Voodoo Miranda said, gesturing at some mounds of wax on the table.

"Work?" Scarlet stepped closer. One of the mounds had a distinct human shape. *A voodoo doll,* she realized, just as Miranda snatched it up and tucked it into her pocket. Scarelt had heard sailors whisper that if you ever needed to get revenge, Voodoo Miranda could help. She'd whip up a little wax doll that looked just like your enemy in the time it took you to say "scalawag." Then she'd stick little pins in the doll's back and ears, and the unfortunate person would be keeling over in no time. Scarlet shivered, feeling invisible pinpricks up and down her spine.

"Sit." Miranda pointed to a chair, and Scarlet obeyed, finding herself staring into the eyes of a frog, floating wide-eyed in a jar of yellow liquid. When Miranda wasn't looking, she quickly turned the jar so the creature was facing away from her.

"Make yourself comfortable," Miranda said.

"Thanks," Scarlet said weakly.

"Ah. That'd be your father," said Miranda.

"Really? I didn't hear anything," Scarlet replied, but Miranda had already slipped back down the hallway.

"Huh," Scarlet muttered, peering into another nearby jar on the counter, which appeared to hold several hundred small green beetles. "What does she *do* with all this stuff, anyway?"

Fortunately, before she could find the answer, the door swung open again, and Admiral McCray walked into the room.

"Scarlet!" He stopped and took off his blue cap, a smile spreading across his face. She stood up and let him pull her into a warm hug. For the tiniest moment, she even let herself relax, enjoying the feeling of having someone take care of her. But then she felt Miranda's eyes on her back, and she wiggled out of her father's arms. The voodoo queen was watching them intently, stroking her python's head.

"Thank you, Miranda," said the admiral. "We won't be long." He pulled out a chair and sat down at the table, dropping his hat between himself and the frog.

Scarlet frowned. How could her father be so comfortable in a place that was so . . . strange?

Miranda nodded. "There are cookies on the counter if you get hungry." She narrowed her eyes at Scarlet. "Looks like you could use a good meal."

"I just ate," Scarlet said quickly, although it had been several hours since she'd snacked on the nuts Jem had packed. If the jars around the kitchen were any indication of the ingredients Miranda baked with, she'd rather pass.

Miranda shrugged and slipped away again, leaving Scarlet and her father alone.

Even now, it still surprised her to see him. Not that he'd changed much in their time apart; she'd known him the moment she saw him on Island X, about a month before. He'd arrived with his men, scouting the island for trees and spices to harvest, and she'd quickly realized that he'd completely forgotten everything about the island—he didn't even recognize it as the place he'd called home for years.

"Please, sit down." He gestured to her chair, and she sat again. He picked up his cap, then set it back down on the table. "So."

"So," she said.

"Are the tree houses finished now?"

"Almost," she replied. "They look jolly—Fitz did a great job."

"And the garden?"

"Done. Gil took a real shine to weeding and planting. Sina thinks we'll have squash in a month or so."

The admiral nodded and fiddled with his cap. "And no sign of that pirate captain . . . what's his name again?"

Scarlet shook her head. The Dread Pirate Captain Wallace Hammerstein-Jones led the *Dark Ranger*, the ship Lucas Lawrence defected to. He was just as treasure hungry as Lucas himself, which meant more trouble for the Lost Souls, since Lucas had Uncle Finn's treasure map. Scarlet tapped her feet on the floor, wondering if either pirate was in port that night and what her crewmates might do if they ran into them. She peered out the cloudy window, hoping her father wouldn't keep her long.

"Speaking of captains," her father continued, "do you have a plan to stop this new one from getting the treasure?"

Scarlet's head snapped back. "What new one?"

The admiral looked down at the frog in the jar and noticed it for the first time. He grimaced and turned it so that it faced the wall.

"The new pirate captain," he repeated. "Surely you've heard of him."

Scarlet shook her head, suddenly grateful for her father's presence in port. This sounded serious.

The admiral frowned. "Everyone's talking about him, though I have yet to meet anyone who has actually met him. Apparently a new pirate is rising to power, and he's gathering a crew of the filthiest and fiercest pirates around. Rumor has it he aims to be the most powerful pirate in all the tropics. They call him the Rebel."

"What?" Scarlet cried, then lowered her voice. "What does that mean?"

"Well, it's someone who defies authority and—"

"I know what *rebel* means," Scarlet snapped. Then she bit her lip. "Sorry. I meant, what does this mean for *us*?"

The admiral frowned. "Well, he wants the most powerful crew, the fastest and biggest ship, and control of all the treasure around."

"Shivers!" Scarlet tried to imagine it. Then she started as another thought came to mind. "What if Lucas decides to join this . . . this Rebel? He's got the map!"

27

"My thoughts exactly," said her father. "He's just the type to—"

Voodoo Miranda poked her head into the kitchen. "Hungry yet?" she asked, narrowing her eyes at Scarlet.

"Oh no!" Scarlet said. "I'm full." She patted her stomach, which proceeded to growl.

"Thought so," Miranda said, sweeping through the door. The striped viper was still nestled in her hair, but the snake on her wrist was nowhere to be seen. Scarlet glanced around nervously and lifted her boots off the floor. "I baked them just last week." Miranda grabbed a plate piled with small gray lumps off the counter and thrust them at Scarlet.

"Oh, I couldn't—"

"Try them!" Miranda pushed the plate toward her.

Scarlet snatched up a gray lump and took a nibble. It tasted salty and a bit like the hardtack the Lost Souls used to eat on board the *Hop*. But there was something else . . . some flavor she couldn't quite put her finger on. "Um . . . what kind of cookie is it?"

Miranda licked her purple lips. "I call it 'rodent surprise.' The snakes love them."

Scarlet's mouth fell open, and she looked down at her half-eaten cookie. Sure enough, the tip of a tiny hairless tail was sticking out. She gagged and sputtered. Miranda was watching her closely, as was the viper in her hair. It took all her will to swallow.

"It's good," Scarlet told them weakly.

Miranda straightened and gave her another wide purple smile. "I know," she said, and slipped back out the door.

Scarlet swallowed hard again and turned back to her father. "Look, as fun as this is, I can't stay much longer. I've got to get back to my crew. We'll need another plan to protect the island from this . . . this Rebel." She stood and pushed back her chair. "Keep notes on everything you hear about him, will you? Then you can fill me in next time I'm in port."

The admiral nodded and checked his pocket watch. "Wait," he said. "There's one more thing."

"About the Rebel?"

"Well, no. This is . . . something different."

Scarlet sat back down and watched him fiddle with his cap again. Could he have even *worse* news? Maybe one of the King's Men had spotted them after their last meeting and guessed her identity. Or maybe they'd guessed what the admiral was up to. Then—

"Your uncle Daniel is coming for a visit. From the Old World."

Scarlet cocked her head to the side. "My what?"

"Your uncle Daniel," he repeated. "My older brother. You've never met him."

"Oh." Scarlet relaxed, relieved that her identity and her father's new mission to protect the Lost Souls and Island X were still secret.

"He won't be staying long. Three weeks at most, and he'll be bringing his daughter, who's about your age. Her name is Josephine."

"I see," Scarlet said, although she didn't see what this news had to do with her.

"Daniel is a very high-ranking King's Man. In fact,

he's a deputy advisor to King Aberhard himself."

"Mmm-hmm."

"When we moved away from the island after the fever, he used his influence to get me a position with the King's Men again. They would have never taken me back otherwise."

"Because, God forbid, you'd gone off and married an Islander," Scarlet finished sarcastically.

The admiral paused. "Daniel means well," he said carefully. "He doesn't understand the tropics. He's only ever advised from afar. But he's my brother, and he's always taken care of me. He was going to take care of you, too, when I wanted to send you back to the Old World. So when you disappeared, I . . . I didn't tell him. I knew he'd be on the first ship over to search for you. It would have turned my family upside down."

This only went to prove Scarlet's theory that grown-ups made no sense. If you couldn't call them for help because they'd only make more trouble, what good were they? But she stayed quiet, a pit beginning to grow in her stomach.

"But now he's coming on business for the king. I'm not sure what it's about, but the point is, he's family."

"And?" Scarlet prodded, not entirely sure she wanted to hear the answer.

"And I need you to come stay with me in port."

Scarlet's mouth fell open. "You *what*?"

The admiral nodded, hardening his jaw as if he were giving orders to another King's Man. "It'll be about three weeks, according to Daniel."

"Three weeks?" Scarlet couldn't believe her ears. "Father, this is absurd! I can't leave the island for three *days,* let alone *weeks*!"

Her father frowned. "Believe me, Scarlet, we have no choice here. I cannot have my brother finding out that you live by yourself on another island with a group of children. He wouldn't understand."

"But—"

"And what's more, it could be dangerous. Daniel's loyalty lies first and foremost with the king, and if he were to find out about Island X and its treasure—the very treasure King Aberhard is looking for—I'd hate to think what he'd have to do."

"But . . . but can't you tell him I'm at boarding school?" she pleaded.

Her father shook his head. "He'd insist we go visit you. He wants to meet you, Scarlet. When you didn't come to the Old World like we'd planned, he was disappointed. He was hoping you could be like a sister to Josephine." The admiral placed his hands, palms down, on the table. "Trust me, Scarlet, I've thought this through. There is no way out of it."

Scarlet fought the rising panic in her throat by swallowing hard. "When are they coming?"

"Their ship docks tomorrow."

"Tomorrow?" she cried. "You've got to be joking! My crew—"

"Will survive without you for three weeks," he interrupted, his voice firm. "They're smart and strong, and nothing will go wrong in your absence."

"But—"

"Scarlet." This time his voice was heavy, and she knew there was no use arguing anymore. "Sometimes we have to do things we don't want. That's what having a family is all about."

And that just absolutely scuttled.

CHAPTER THREE

"Three *weeks*?" Jem repeated, certain he couldn't have heard her correctly.

Scarlet looked as if she wasn't sure whether to smack someone or burst into tears. "Three weeks," she said hopelessly.

It was now after midnight, and the Lost Souls stood on the dock near their rowboat. Nothing but a slender crescent moon illuminated the crew's faces, but Jem could see the shock on each one.

"But . . . but what'll we do without you?" Edwin asked, wide-eyed. "Anything can happen in three weeks! Think of how much has happened since we got to the island!"

"The *Dark Ranger* pirates invaded twice," Emmett pointed out.

"Then the King's Men came," Edwin added.

"And killed that smelly wild pig. Then—"

"So you'll be hosting Old World relatives?" Jem cut the twins off before Scarlet threw herself right into the ocean.

Scarlet wrung her hands. "Can you believe it? I'm going to have to spend three weeks showing my stuffy Uncle Daniel around skuzzy old Port Aberhard. And his niece, too. *Josephine*." She said the name as if it tasted like slimy oysters.

Jem couldn't help but feel a bit sorry for Josephine, whoever she was. She had no idea what she was in for.

"Sink me." Scarlet suddenly turned pale. "I'm going to have dress up, aren't I?" She turned to Jem, eyes wide. "I hadn't thought of that. I'm going to have to wear a dress! And *petticoats*! *Blast*!" She shook her fist at the moon, nearly punching Edwin in the head.

Jem turned away for a moment, to sort things out in his brain. It was a perplexing situation, no doubt. But it wouldn't be the first time Scarlet had left him in charge. He'd had to lead the crew several times in the past few weeks while she'd been off chasing an irritated monkey or an ara with indigestion. It had been tricky at first, getting them to listen to him, but now it was easier, especially after he'd overseen the tree house–building project. Three weeks was a long time, though.

I'll be Deputy Captain, he thought, then brightened. *That's a good title. Maybe I can handle this.* And he turned back to Scarlet to tell her so.

"And I'll have to comb my hair," Scarlet was saying. "And use those . . . those things to eat with," she went on. "What're they called again, Fitz?"

"Cutlery," Jem said.

"Exactly." Scarlet nodded. "I *detest* cutlery. Knives are for cutting off pirates' noses, not buttering bread."

"But what about the panther?" Edwin asked. "How are we going to fend it off without you?"

Jem's stomach dropped. He'd forgotten about the panther.

Scarlet paused and stared at Edwin. Then she shook

her head. "You're right. I can't do it. I can't stay here. I'll go tell him right now."

"Wait." Jem reached out and laid a hand on her arm. "You have to," he said, sounding a hundred times more certain than he felt. "Your father's right—you have to keep up appearances so your uncle doesn't find out about the island. You'll . . . you'll be protecting it, in a way," he added.

She didn't look convinced. And frankly, neither was he. Now that he thought about it, it wasn't just the panther that stood to cause him trouble. He couldn't understand the other animals like Scarlet could— suppose they needed to tell him about an intruder? And communicating with the Islanders was no picnic, either. Only Scarlet knew how to do those things.

"Well, it scuttles for sure," Tim finally spoke up. "But it might actually be helpful."

Scarlet looked at him incredulously. "How could it *possibly* be helpful?"

"Well, Liam and I heard a nasty rumor while we were stealing daggers from some swabs' boots. Didn't we, Liam?"

Liam nodded. "We didn't hear the whole story, but it sounds like there's a new captain sailing around, and he's going to be trouble."

"I heard that, too," Smitty said.

Scarlet snapped her fingers. "That's right! My father told me about him, but I completely forgot about it after he told me the other news."

"What's this? What's going on?" Jem demanded.

He hadn't heard anything about a pirate captain while searching for the hooks and nails he needed for the tree houses.

"Some pirate's determined to be the most powerful in all the tropics," Scarlet told him. "They call him the Rebel, and he wants the fastest ship and all the treasure around. And he's gathering a crew of the dirtiest scoundrels to back him up."

"Like Pegleg Ted," said Tim. "And Deadeye Johnny. You remember old Deadeye, Jem?"

Jem's stomach dropped down to his toes. "How could I forget?" He'd once stolen a silver and ivory–handled pocketknife from Deadeye Johnny, before learning that the pirate was one of the fiercest around. Deadeye had chased him around port, threatening to cut off his nose, and Jem didn't doubt for a moment that he'd do it, even now.

"Which is why I can't be stuck in port," Scarlet said, just as Tim concluded, "Which is why you need to be in port."

"What?" Scarlet spun toward him. "Swig, are you crazy?"

"We need a spy." Tim straightened his spectacles. "We need someone to find out everything they can about this new captain."

Jem nodded. Tim had a point. "That way, we'll be two steps ahead of him if he finds out about the treasure. He'll never take us by surprise, and you'll be protecting the island from afar," Jem finished, now far more convinced in his logic.

Scarlet thought about this for a moment, then agreed that it made sense. "But I don't see why it has to be me. Emmett could do it. Or Edwin."

"Doubt I could pass for the admiral's daughter," Emmett quipped.

"I'd look terrible in a dress," added Edwin.

Scarlet groaned. "I'll look just as bad!"

"Not possible," said Smitty. "Have you seen Ed's legs?"

"Hey now!" Edwin protested.

"Captain, come on," Jem cut in. "It won't be that bad." Actually, a few weeks in port with square meals and a real bed sounded like a nice holiday to him. The admiral probably even had a library in his quarters. If there was one thing Jem missed about the Old World, it was reading before bed at night. He briefly thought about asking Scarlet to steal him a book or two, then decided it wasn't the time.

Scarlet shook her head. "Oh, it'll be bad, all right," she growled. "It'll absolutely scuttle."

Jem opened his mouth to protest again, but she cut him off.

"But I'll do it for the island," she said. "On one condition."

"What?" asked Jem.

"That none of you lunkheads say the word *dress* again till I'm gone."

"Hey, Fitz, wanna see what I got for Sina?" Smitty

asked Jem once they'd weighed anchor and begun to sail for home. After finally bidding Scarlet farewell, they'd rowed back out to the *Hop* and tried to get a few hours of sleep before sunrise. Jem had failed miserably, and he could tell by their droopy eyes the others had as well.

Jem looked up from the sail he was mending, sitting cross-legged on the fo'c'sle. He shaded his eyes from the sun. "You found a gift, then?"

Smitty nodded, crouching down beside him and digging in his pocket. "Whaddya think?" He pulled out a hair clip made from a tortoise shell. "Nice, hey? I think it's supposed to look something like this." Smitty snapped the clip around a bunch of his hair, so that it spouted like a dirty blond fountain off the crown of his head. "Except nicer. Sina's hair is much nicer." A dreamy look spread over his face.

Jem tried not to laugh. "It's, um, nice," he said. "But Smitty, think for a moment. What's the most important thing in the world to Sina?"

Smitty thought about this, then concluded, "Kapu."

"True," Jem admitted. "But other than her brother. What's the second most important thing to her?"

"Um . . ." Smitty thought again. "The island, maybe? She's big on nature."

"Exactly." Jem looked pointedly at the clip.

Smitty untangled it from his hair and looked from the clip to Jem and back again. "I don't get it."

Jem sighed. "Smit, someone offed a tortoise to make that."

Smitty's mouth fell open, and he dropped the clip.

"You're right! Blimey, Sina would *hate* that." He looked at Jem. "Wow, you saved my hide, Fitz. Thanks a million. But what am I going to get her now?"

Fortunately, before Jem could begin brainstorming gift ideas, Tim began shouting from the ship's wheel.

"All hands on deck!" he hollered. "Mysterious vessel, dead ahead!"

Jem and Smitty scrambled to their feet and ran over to the wheel. Liam, Emmett, and Edwin were already there, pointing at something in the distance. Tim dug the spyglass out of his pocket and raised it to his eye.

"What is it?" Jem squinted. He could just make out a tiny black dot on the horizon.

"What the flotsam?" Tim murmured. He lowered the spyglass and handed it to Jem without taking his eyes off the speck in the distance. "You're not going to believe this."

Jem pressed the spyglass to his eye. It took a moment for him to find the boat, which turned out to be even smaller than he'd thought. In fact, it was tiny.

"Is it . . . a dinghy?"

"In the middle of the ocean?" said Liam.

"Look closer," said Tim.

Jem stared harder at the tiny bobbing boat, until the two passengers inside it came into view. Both were sunburned to a crisp, as if they'd been adrift on the open ocean for days. One—a tall man with a red bandana wrapped around his head—had a single oar. The other man was wearing a tattered coat several sizes too big for him. He seemed to be directing the man with the oar, who looked ready to throw him overboard.

"What is it?" Edwin tugged on Jem's shirtsleeve. "*Who* is it?"

Jem lowered the spyglass and looked at Tim, whose incredulous expression, he guessed, mirrored his own. "It's . . . it's . . ."

"Exactly," said Tim.

"But *how* . . . ?"

"No idea." Tim turned the wheel, steering them toward the dinghy. "But we're going to have to find out."

The Lost Souls hauled the Dread Pirate Captain Wallace Hammerstein-Jones and his right-hand man, Iron "Pete" Morgan, out of their dinghy and onto the *Hop*. The pirates flopped onto the main deck like fresh-caught flounder, gasping for water. Liam tossed them each a canteen.

Edwin tied their rowboat to the bow of the ship, and Smitty bound their hands and feet. Pete and Captain Wallace might have been in trouble, but they were still enemies of the Lost Souls. The last time Jem had seen them, in fact, they'd been trying to steal the treasure. Fortunately, the Lost Souls had been able to chase them off before they could spot any rubies.

The pirates guzzled their water until Jem began to wonder if they might burst. Finally, Captain Wallace set down his canteen and took a long, deep breath. He looked around him, his rodent eyes taking in each of his captors one at a time. "Phooey," he said.

Smitty unsheathed his cutlass and pointed it right between the captain's eyes. "Well, Cap'n," he said cheerfully. "Long time, no see."

Captain Wallace groaned and squeezed his eyes shut.

"Aw, don't be like that," said Smitty. "We've got so much to catch up on. Look, I'll start. Let me tell you all about the girl I love."

The captain groaned again and covered his face with his bound hands.

"All right, then." Smitty *tsk*ed. "*You* start. Tell us how you and your man ended up in a dinghy in the middle of the sea."

Tim prodded the captain's boot with his toe. "Come on. Out with it."

"I'll explain." Pete set his canteen aside. "Thanks for that, by the way. Always knew you young'uns weren't such a bad lot."

Jem raised an eyebrow. Pete was smarter than most pirates, but he still wasn't to be trusted.

Captain Wallace glared at him, but Pete ignored him. "Too bad I can't say the same for your former crewmate," he continued. "He's the reason we were out there for days, with no water and barely a speck of food."

"What?" Jem said. "What did you say?"

"There would have been more than a speck if you hadn't dropped the hardtack overboard," Captain Wallace muttered.

"Look, I said I was sorry, didn't I?" Pete looked as if he'd had to restrain himself many a time from dropping the captain overboard, too.

"*Sorry* isn't good enough, butterfingers!" cried Captain Wallace.

"Wait!" Jem yelled. "What are you talking about? Do you mean Lucas?"

Smitty turned his cutlass on Pete. "What about Lucas?" he asked. "What happened?"

"The blasted little biscuit-eater mutinied!" Captain Wallace cried. "On me! The Dread Pirate Captain Wallace Hammerstein-Jones! Terror of the Seven Seas! Feared by sailors from one shore to—"

"Right, we get it." Smitty silenced him by pointing his cutlass back between the captain's eyes. "What about Lucas?"

"Lucas Lawrence convinced nearly every pirate on board the *Dark Ranger* to turn against the captain and follow him instead." Pete gritted his teeth. "Stupid child. I knew ever since I laid eyes on him that he'd only be trouble."

"Oh no," Jem whispered as his stomach plummeted.

"Oh, you did, did you?" Captain Wallace sneered at Pete. "Then why didn't you say so?"

"Say so!" Pete cried. "I *said so* every day, at least a dozen times. You didn't listen!"

Captain Wallace opened his mouth to respond but couldn't seem to come up with a good argument. "Anyway," he huffed, "Lucas and his crew took off with the ship, leaving us the bloody dinghy and *one* oar. Me! In a dinghy! The Dread Pirate Captain Wallace Hammerstein-Jones! Terror of the—"

"We get it!" the boys cried in unison, and Captain Wallace fell silent with a pout.

Jem turned to his crewmates, who looked as stunned as he felt.

"So Lucas is the new captain of the *Dark Ranger*?" Emmett asked.

Jem nodded, thinking hard. Lucas had taken a great risk, angering Captain Wallace. He must have been confident in his new allies. Or maybe, knowing the boy's hunger for treasure, he'd just gotten sick of seeing someone else take the lion's share of the spoils. On most ships, the captain took half of whatever the crew plundered. Either way, this meant big trouble— enormous trouble, even—since Lucas knew exactly where to find the greatest treasure around.

Tim shook his head. "Lucas is the last swab alive who should have control of a ship."

"Let alone the entire tropics," Pete added.

All heads swung toward him.

"The . . . *what*?" Jem said.

Pete took one last swig of his water, draining his canteen. "The entire tropics," he repeated, wiping his mouth on his sleeve. "Surely you've heard of the Rebel?"

"Yes, but—" Jem fell silent as he realized what Pete was saying.

"That'd be Lucas."

CHAPTER FOUR

"All good pirates come to order!"

The Lost Souls gathered in front of Jem, stopped whispering among themselves, and looked at him expectantly, their faces illuminated by firefly lanterns. All had just learned that their captain would be away for several weeks *and* that their sworn enemy was planning to take over the tropics. A few of them gnawed on dirty fingernails. A few more had eyes the size of guava fruit.

Jem's knees wobbled. It had been a very, *very* long day. After interrogating the former *Dark Ranger* pirates and learning the terrible news, he and the crew had sailed back to Island X, then slogged through the jungle for five hours to reach the rest of the Lost Souls. Thankfully, no one had been eaten up by a panther in their absence.

While Tim and Smitty spread the news and gathered everyone for a meeting, Jem took a moment to compose his thoughts. Something had been nagging at his brain since they'd set the pirates adrift in their dinghy again. Why *did* Lucas want to be the most powerful pirate in the tropics? He was treasure-hungry, of course, but was that all? Somehow, Jem thought not. He needed time and space to ponder it, though. And just then, he had a meeting to lead.

He sighed. All he really wanted to do was curl up in bed and forget everything that had happened—a *real*

bed, with a blanket and pillow. And a good book, too, like one of the adventure novels he used to read back in the Old World. Those were the days—when he could read about adventure without having to live it.

"So the captain's really staying in port to be with some Old Worlders?" a boy named Monty asked in disbelief.

Jem nodded. "She had no choice. Her uncle's a high-ranking King's Man, and they couldn't have him getting suspicious. If he found out about Island X, there'd be trouble."

The Lost Souls exchanged uncertain glances.

"It's going to be okay, though," he added, assuming a brave face. "We'll be fine here without her for a few weeks. I'll be your Deputy Captain."

"Our what?" asked Gil.

"It's like a substitute captain," Jem explained. "Just a title."

"Oh."

"And what about Lucas?" Ronagh elbowed her way to the front of the crowd. A small black monkey perched on her shoulder—Jem recognized it as the troublesome one Kapu kept as a pet. Its hands were tangled in Ronagh's hair, and its eyes were wide like everyone else's. "Did he really mutiny against the Dread Captain Hammer–What's-his-name?"

Jem nodded, struggling to maintain his brave face. "That's what Pete and Captain Wallace told us. He aims to have the biggest ship, the fiercest crew, and control of all the treasure in the tropics. They're calling him the Rebel."

"What's a rebel?" Ronagh wrinkled her nose.

"Someone who won't listen to authority," said Jem.

"Well, they got that part right," Ronagh told the monkey on her shoulder, who tugged on her earlobe.

"But he's only thirteen," Elmo pointed out. "Why would they follow him?"

Tim shrugged. "No one in port seems to know that. In fact, Liam and I heard some merchants say that the earth shakes when he walks."

"A cabin boy told me that if he looks at you, you'd better run and hide," Edwin added.

"Maybe when they actually see him, they won't be so scared?" Elmo said hopefully.

Smitty shook his head. "You know Lucas. He could pass for sixteen, maybe even older." He took a step closer to Sina and tried once again to put a protective arm around her, but she shrugged him off.

Jem wished Scarlet were there to make sure Sina and Kapu understood what was going on. He'd tried his best to act it out for them when they'd arrived for the meeting, but he wasn't sure how effective his imitation of pirates cowering in Lucas's presence had been.

"I bet he'll steal a big old schooner," said Charlie.

Tim shook his head. "He wouldn't settle for anything less than a man-o'-war."

"Bet he won't even settle for hardtack on board," cried Sam.

"Yeah," said Emmett. "It'll be only roast chicken and pudding for Lucas."

"Or pudding for every meal!" cried Elmo.

Jem's stomach growled, and he tried not to think about pudding.

"I'll bet he gets a real intimidating uniform," said Smitty, who loved a good uniform. "Something sleek, I bet. Maybe silver or gold," he added wistfully.

"The Rebel." Tim shook his head in disgust. "I can think of a better word for him."

"Yeah!" Liam piped up. "Like—"

"We all know he's a biscuit-eater," Jem cut in, although he expected Liam had something worse in mind. "But the fact remains that we've got trouble on our hands. We don't know when Lucas is going to show up with his new crew, but we know he will eventually. Scarlet will be spying in port, learning all she can about his plan. And hopefully, she'll be back in time for us to scuttle it."

The Lost Souls nodded.

"I hate to say it, but we've got more trouble than that," Gil spoke up, stepping to the front of the crowd. Never a particularly clean pirate, Gil was now permanently covered in dirt from the garden.

"What now?" Jem sighed. He couldn't take much more bad news.

"I saw a track this morning, near the squash garden. A big track—bigger than any I've ever seen."

"You mean . . ." Jem couldn't even bring himself to say it.

Gil shrugged. "I've never seen a panther track before, but this ain't no smelly wild pig."

"I heard a howl in the middle of the night," Sam

47

added. "At first I thought it was Charlie having a nightmare, but he says it wasn't."

"It *wasn't*," Charlie insisted.

"Right." Jem took a deep breath, trying to keep his thoughts straight. "Well, I'm going to start building doors on the tree houses, to reinforce them. Who'll help me?" Three boys raised their hands, and he nodded, thankful that at least the crew was cooperating with their Deputy Captain. The island was giving him plenty to worry about without them.

"Tim. Liam. You still awake?"

"Mmph," came the mumbled reply.

"Smitty?"

"No. Go to sleep."

Jem sat up in his hammock and reached for his lantern. He gave it a shake, and the fireflies awoke, flickering sleepily. *Sorry,* he told them silently. *But this is important.*

"I've been thinking," he began.

"Look, Fitz, I know you're all about this thinking thing, but it's the middle of the night," said Smitty. "I barely slept last night, and I can't keep my eyes open. Can we talk in the morning?"

Liam mumbled in agreement.

"This'll just take a minute. Swig? You awake?"

"Unfortunately," Tim grumbled. "What is it?"

"I need you to tell me what you heard people saying about Lucas in port."

Tim sighed and sat up. "I told you already."

"Tell me again," Jem insisted.

"That merchant said that he heard the earth shakes when Lucas walks," said Tim.

"Mm-hm." Jem nodded. "What else?"

Smitty flopped onto his side to face them. "I heard an old toothless sea dog say that the captain was sneaky—he'd steal everything you own, and you'd never notice nothing."

"Anything," Jem corrected him.

"Fitz, if you're going to correct my grammar in the middle of the night, I might have to clock you one."

"Sorry," Jem said quickly. "But was there anything else? Anything about *why* he wants to be the most powerful captain in the tropics?"

"What captain wouldn't?" Smitty yawned. "You'd never have to worry about anyone raiding your ship or stealing your men. You'd have all the money you wanted, and no one to answer to."

"True, but . . ." Jem tapped the lantern, thinking hard.

"A barmaid in the tavern said he planned to fill his big old ship with servants," Liam mumbled.

Jem stopped tapping. "What?"

Liam yawned and stretched. "More than just the odd cabin boy, she said. These would be slaves, forced to do all the worst and most dangerous jobs, like scaling to the crow's nest in a hurricane. And cleaning the long drop for eternity."

Jem looked up at Liam, then over at Smitty and Tim. "Uh-oh," they all said together.

"You think . . ." Tim began.

"That's us?" Smitty finished.

Jem nodded. "Scarlet shamed Lucas. Remember how she left him on the Island of Smelly Wild Pigs when he stole my knife? This isn't about the treasure. It's about—"

"Revenge," Tim finished.

Smitty gave a low whistle, and even Liam sat up, now fully awake.

Jem nodded. "Lucas is going to make us pay."

CHAPTER FIVE

Scarlet awoke to a strange sound. In the darkness of her room, she listened hard for a minute before realizing that what she was hearing was nothing.

Absolutely nothing.

There were no aras squawking good morning. No bugs buzzing around her ears. No sleepy murmurs from Ronagh, one hammock away. She was completely, utterly alone.

Also, she was very warm, flattened between a heavy blanket and a soft mattress. In fact, she was almost . . . cozy. It felt completely unnatural.

She flung off her blanket and jumped out of bed, feeling her way through the darkness to the small window between the two beds the admiral had set up for herself and Josephine. She'd noticed it when she'd arrived the night before but had been too exhausted to look out. She felt around for the shutters, then yanked them open, flooding the tiny bedroom with morning light.

She'd desperately hoped the window would look out to sea, maybe even give a view of Island X, but no such luck. She could only see the street below, which even now was bustling with merchants heading to the docks to hawk their wares. A horse clopped by pulling a cart full of limes and papayas, its hooves caked with red mud. A rooster strutted across the street, followed by a maid cursing it for escaping its pen.

Scarlet shut her eyes. She'd survived her first night in the admiral's house, in the middle of Port Aberhard and miles from her home. *Just twenty more nights to go, give or take,* she told herself. *I can do that, right?*

Someone knocked on the door, and before she could holler that she wasn't yet decent, the door swung open and in marched one of her father's maids. A short, round woman with flyaway blond curls and a long gray dress, she gave Scarlet a once-over and tutted softly. Dressed in only a nightgown, Scarlet reddened and folded her arms across her chest.

"Aren't ye a skinny little thing," the woman commented. "Don't they feed ye at that boarding school of yers?"

"Um . . . ," Scarlet began. Her father had warned her that everyone in the house believed she went to a little-known boarding school on one of the islands, but she hadn't had a chance to invent some lies about it herself. She tried to remember what Jem had said about his boarding school back in the Old World. Something about football and libraries and a boring old headmaster? Whatever he'd said, it had sounded truly awful.

"Never mind," the maid said cheerily. "Breakfast'll be ready in no time. I'm Meggie, by the way. I heard ye need some clothes, so I brought a few things ye might like." She produced an armload of dresses, and Scarlet cringed. "How about this one?" Meggie held up a butter-yellow eyesore, all ribbons and frills. Scarlet could practically feel the lace scratching her neck and the satiny fabric damp against her back, just by looking at it. She had half a mind to fling herself out the window.

"Maybe something more . . . simple?" she croaked.

"Hmm." Meggie picked through the pile. "So it's simple ye want. How's this?" She held up a blue dress, which still had ribbons and frills, but not quite as many. "Simplest I've got here."

Scarlet bit her lip. "All right."

Meggie laid the dress on the bed next to the petticoats Scarlet would have to wear under it.

She stood for a moment, staring at her new clothes, completely at a loss as to how to get into them. Finally, she swallowed her pride, feeling her ears turn crimson. "Um, can you . . . help me? I . . . um . . . I'm only used to wearing my school uniform. Which is . . . different."

Meggie gave her an odd look but didn't say anything. She hung up the other dresses, then turned her attention to Scarlet. She pulled one layer of clothing after another over Scarlet's head, buttoning, clasping, and cinching everything in place.

"My, yer a squirmy one!" Meggie gasped as she pulled on the laces at the back of the dress. "It's like ye've never worn a dress before!"

"Blimey!" Scarlet cried as Meggie gave the laces an especially hard yank. "Sorry," she said quickly, remembering her place. "It's just . . . does it have to be so *tight*?" She was already gasping for breath, and she had yet to leave the bedroom.

Fifteen minutes later, Scarlet was fully dressed in

petticoats, dress, boots, and stockings, and Meggie was damp with sweat and out of breath.

"There now. That's better." Meggie wiped her forehead.

"Is it?" Scarlet muttered. It certainly didn't feel better. In fact, it had never felt worse. Her laces were so tight and her boots so pinchy that she couldn't run if her life depended on it. But she swallowed her curses and thanked Meggie, anyway. She'd probably need the maid's help again.

Meggie nodded. "Go on, now. Yer father'll be in the library. I'll bring yer breakfast there."

Scarlet nodded and left the bedroom, walking bowlegged thanks to her bunchy petticoats and wobbling on the small heels of her boots. How was she ever going to fool Uncle Daniel and Josephine into thinking she was a proper young lady?

She found her father in his library, sipping tea while studying a map on the desk. He choked when he saw her, and set down his teacup.

"Don't even say it," Scarlet snapped.

"You look nice," he insisted. "Just a bit . . . unnatural." The corners of his eyes crinkled, and a smile tugged at his mouth.

Scarlet ignored him, turning away to get a good look at the room. It was just what she would have expected from a King's Man's library. The enormous shelves packed with leather-bound books would have made Jem swoon. The admiral's desk was piled high with maps and measuring instruments that Scarlet had never seen before. And all the furniture in the room was made of dark red wood—island trees, no doubt. Scarlet reached out to touch the smooth grain, then thought better of it and drew back.

Meggie entered, carrying a tray. She set it down on a table by the window. "Yer breakfast, miss." Then she winked at Scarlet and left the room.

Scarlet sat before the toast the maid had buttered and sprinkled with cinnamon, and for a moment she wished she could package it up and send it to Jem. But since that wasn't an option, she wolfed down an entire slice in two bites. Then she dumped two spoonfuls of sugar into her tea and gulped it down.

"Good?" Her father raised his eyebrows.

"Not bad." And it wasn't. Though she'd rather have been eating with her crew back in the clearing, there was something to be said for a hot breakfast. She wiped her buttery fingers on her dress.

He sighed and walked over to the table. "Etiquette Rule Number One," he said. "Don't wipe your hands on your clothes." He handed her a cloth. "And remember to chew before you swallow. You no longer have to compete with twenty-three other pirates for food."

Scarlet crumpled the cloth and dropped it in her lap. She hated rules. At least, ones she didn't make up herself. She picked up the other slice of toast and bit into it, forcing herself to chew slowly.

Her father sat down across from her and poured himself more tea. As he reached for the milk, Scarlet caught sight of a leather cord around his neck.

"What's that?" she asked, mouth full.

"Swallow first, then talk."

She rolled her eyes and swallowed.

"And no eye-rolling, Scarlet. You've got to pass for an educated young lady."

She bristled but held her tongue.

He pulled on the cord, revealing a wooden star on the end. "Remember this?"

Scarlet nodded. "Of course." It was one of the little stars he'd carved for her when they still lived with the Islanders. Sina had given it to Scarlet when they'd been reunited. And Scarlet had passed it on to her father to jog his memories of their life together before her mother died.

She watched him tuck the star back into his shirt. *He's on your side*, she reminded herself. *He's fighting for the island, too.*

"All right." She sighed, wiping her hands on the cloth. "Tell me about these relatives. Uncle Daniel and Josephine. Think she'd let me call her Jo?"

Her father gave her a wry smile. "I rather doubt it." He sipped his tea, then set it down again. "Daniel is my only brother," he began. "He's five years older than me. After our father died when I was around your age, Daniel looked out for me like a father would. He became a King's Man, and when I turned eighteen, he insisted they accept me as well."

Scarlet nodded. "And Josephine? What do you know about her?"

He shook his head. "Not much. She's your age and

56

goes to a prestigious boarding school for young ladies. I'm not quite sure why Daniel's bringing her along. Perhaps to broaden her horizons."

Scarlet poured herself more tea and spooned more sugar into it. "We're going to have nothing in common."

"Well, actually, you do have one big thing in common," he told her. "Josephine lost her mother to an illness, too. Just last year."

"She did?" Scarlet looked up at her father, who nodded. "Oh." She stirred her tea, unsure how that would make them better friends. Would she even want to bring it up?

"Admiral McCray, sir." Meggie poked her head through the door.

The admiral looked up. "Yes, Meggie?"

"Beg yer pardon, but I'm to tell ye that the schooner yer waiting for is pulling into port. Yer guests have arrived."

The admiral dabbed at his mouth with a cloth. "Yes, that'll be them. Thank you, Meggie." He stood and looked down at Scarlet. "Ready?"

She tossed back her tea and grimaced at the thought of standing in her pinchy boots.

"It's only a few weeks, Scarlet," her father reminded her. "And maybe you'll find your own horizons broadening as well. Now, shall we?"

By the time they arrived at the docks, a crowd had already gathered. The giant schooner had dropped anchor, but its passengers had yet to disembark. The ship towered over the crowd, red and blue flags sagging in the still, humid air as if the journey had tired them right out.

Scarlet glanced down at her dress and noticed a big smear of dirt on the skirt. "Blast!" She rubbed at the stain but only succeeded in spreading it around.

"Scarlet!" Her father glanced down and did a double take. "How did you manage that so quickly?" he whispered.

Scarlet grunted in response, rubbing even harder. "Oh blast, bilge, and blimey! It's in there for good!" She looked up to see a woman in a spotless white dress giving her an alarmed look. She returned a dagger glare, and the woman *tsk*ed and moved away.

"Rule Number Two," her father murmured. "No cursing. I mean it."

"Blast." Scarlet sighed. That was going to be a hard one.

"They're coming!" someone yelled, and everyone looked up to see the schooner's passengers streaming off the ship. The crowd parted to let them pass. A group of ladies in frilly dresses flounced by first, followed by some King's Men smoothing their rumpled uniforms. Then came a mob of merchants wrestling with trunks of wares.

"There!" Admiral McCray cried. "There they are!" He pointed to a pair walking slowly down the ramp. The man had brown hair like Scarlet's father, but his was streaked with gray. He was also a few inches shorter, and judging by his ample belly, better fed. A small, slender girl with chestnut curls and very pale skin clung to his arm.

"Daniel!" her father shouted. "Over here!"

Daniel searched the crowd until he found his brother. Then he waved back. The girl pulled out a pink fan and waved it in front of her face.

"Scurvy," Scarlet said under her breath.

"Come, Scarlet." Admiral McCray pulled her closer to the dock to meet their guests. "Daniel!" He threw his arms around his brother. "It's been so long! Why, you haven't aged a bit. All right, maybe a bit." He tousled his brother's hair.

"I think it looks distinguished." Uncle Daniel laughed.

Scarlet stood a few steps behind her father, watching. It was odd to see him with his brother. Until then, she'd never actually envisioned him as anything but a dull grown-up, but at one time, he and Uncle Daniel must have run around and played games and wreaked havoc like the Lost Souls.

"Father," the girl clinging to Uncle Daniel's sleeve whispered, still fanning her face.

"Oh!" her father exclaimed, as though he'd momentarily forgotten her. "John, this is my daughter, Josephine."

Josephine dipped into a curtsy.

"Wonderful to meet you, my dear," said the admiral. "Are you not feeling well?"

"She's feeling rather faint," Uncle Daniel answered. "Josephine has a weak constitution at the best of times, and two months at sea did nothing to improve it, I'm afraid."

Josephine looked down at her feet. "I'll be all right once I sit down awhile," she said softly.

Scarlet sighed. She didn't know what a constitution was, but she was fairly certain cousin Josephine would not make for a fun companion. She could barely catch her breath standing still, and her arms looked like they could be snapped in two.

"Of course," the admiral said quickly. "We'll head right home, where you can rest up. This is my daughter, Scarlet. I think she and Josephine are going to get along swimmingly." He gave Scarlet a nudge, and she realized that this was her cue to curtsy.

The only problem was, she didn't remember how. Trying to picture how Josephine had done it, she set one foot in front of the other and bent her knees as deeply as she dared. But on her way back up, her ankle twisted, and she had to hop on one foot to regain her balance. Unfortunately, she hopped too far to the left, right onto the foot of a passing boy.

"Ow!" he cried, whirling around to face her. And Scarlet gasped as she found herself nose-to-chest with none other than Lucas Lawrence.

He seemed even taller and broader than the last time she'd seen him, only a few weeks before. Or maybe he was just holding himself taller, with an air of confidence that made her want to reach up and wring his thick neck. A flush crept up the back of her own neck and out to her ears.

For a moment, Lucas just looked down at her. Then he cleared his throat. "Beg your pardon, miss," he said in an unnaturally deep voice. "That was my fault. Are you all right?"

Scarlet's mouth fell open. The bilge rat didn't recognize her!

"You're not hurt?" He smoothed his dirty hair with a big, meaty hand.

Scarlet opened her mouth to answer, then snapped it shut before the curses could escape. Fortunately, her father reached over and put an arm around her.

"She's just fine, thank you," he said, pulling her closer to him.

Lucas looked up at the admiral and stared at him, as if trying to place him. For a moment, Scarlet held her breath, desperately hoping he wouldn't put two and two together. But Lucas shrugged and turned away.

With a sigh of relief, Scarlet and her father turned back to Daniel and Josephine, who seemed too preoccupied with Josephine's weak constitution to have noticed the awkward exchange.

"Well," Scarlet said. "Shall we go home?"

"Let's." Her father offered her his arm, motioning for a man lugging Daniel's and Josephine's trunks to follow.

"Scarlet," Uncle Daniel said as they walked, "your father tells me you attend a fine little boarding school here in the tropics. You and Josephine will have to swap notes. She just started finishing school back home. In fact, before we left, she received an award for being the cleanest and tidiest girl in her year."

"You don't say," Scarlet replied, trying her best to sound impressed. She'd never heard of finishing school before, but if they handed out awards for cleanliness, she wouldn't last a week. She looked down at the stain on her skirt and wondered if Josephine had noticed it.

"You'll have such a pleasant time, you two," Daniel went on. "Josephine has all kinds of interests. Crochet, knitting, embroidery . . ."

"Isn't that nice?" Scarlet's father commented, tightening his grip on Scarlet's arm to remind her of their agreement. "Scarlet enjoys those things, too."

"Can't get enough of them," Scarlet agreed through clenched teeth.

And so began the longest three weeks of her entire life.

CHAPTER SIX

"No one has ever identified the bromeliad that cures androgenetic alopecia," Uncle Finn called to Jem over his shoulder as they wove their way through the jungle, around huge clumps of ferns and over fallen logs, skirting trees with trunks so big that Jem's, Thomas's, and Uncle Finn's arms together wouldn't encircle them. Thomas was out front, trying to clear the way without disturbing too many plants. "So that means," Uncle Finn continued, "it hasn't yet been named."

"Hmm." Jem tried his best to sound interested. Bromeliads were to Uncle Finn what ships were to Tim and animals were to Ronagh. They weren't for him, though. Try as he might, he couldn't muster enthusiasm for any plants at all. The only reason why he was out with the explorers as they searched for samples was because he needed to find Sina and Kapu and didn't want to walk through the jungle alone, lest a panther or a pirate leap out and attack him.

"So, what do you think?" Uncle Finn turned to face him.

"Sorry, what?" Jem ground to a stop.

Uncle Finn sighed. "The name! When I present this new specimen to the High Commission on Neotropical Plantlife, I'll need to name it."

"I know!" Thomas turned around. "How about

Henry? I've always liked the name Henry."

Uncle Finn rolled his eyes to the treetops. "Its genus is *Bediotropicanus*. So it needs a Latin species name. Like *Bediotropicanus onicus,* the one that temporarily erases one's memory."

"Right," said Jem. They'd fed that one to Lucas, Pete, and Captain Wallace after foiling their last attempt to find the treasure. "And . . ." He thought hard, trying to remember the other plant Uncle Finn had found. *"Bediotropicanus plumpicus!"*

"The one that turns hair green," Thomas said.

"Feathers too," Jem added. The Lost Souls had used that one to hide the aras from the pirates. It was a good solution, and one they could use again if the pirates showed up. But if Lucas wanted to harm the Lost Souls, they'd need more than bromeliads to fend him off.

Jem sighed. This Deputy Captain role had become very complicated.

"Exactly," said Uncle Finn. "I'll need such a Latin name for this new species, too."

"How 'bout *Bediotropicanus henry*?" Thomas suggested, stooping to watch a tiny snake slither by his boots.

Uncle Finn did not look impressed. "I was thinking," he said testily, "about naming it after the scientist who'd discovered it."

"Ah," Thomas said to the snake. "Can't be Henry, then." He looked up at Uncle Finn. "Unless your name's actually Henry?"

"So then," Jem cut in before Uncle Finn could

explode, "*Bediotropicanus . . . finnaeus?*"

Uncle Finn straightened and flicked his hair over his shoulder. "Precisely. What do you think?"

"Sounds good," said Jem, although he wondered if it was entirely fair, when Thomas had played an important role in finding the plant as well. In fact, everyone on Island X owed Thomas heaps of thanks, since he'd defected from the *Dark Ranger* pirates to join the Lost Souls as an honorary member.

"That's a nice name, too," Thomas said, straightening and scratching his chest. "So, what'll it be like, visitin' the High Comm . . . Commis . . ."

"High Commission on Neotropical Plantlife." Uncle Finn fell in line behind him again. "I've never appeared before this commission, but I'm sure it will be the experience of a lifetime. I'll have to make a formal presentation and display all my specimens and—"

"Wait." Jem stopped scanning the trees for feline forms as a thought occurred to him. "The High Commission on Neotropical Plantlife is back in the Old World."

"Obviously," Uncle Finn replied without looking back at his nephew.

"And you'll be presenting there . . . when exactly?"

"As soon as possible." Uncle Finn paused to examine a tiny purple bromeliad sprouting off a branch. He snapped off a leaf and tucked it in his bag of samples.

"Which means," Jem concluded, "we'll be going home."

It wasn't a complete surprise, really. When Uncle Finn had shown up at the King's Cross School for Boys to whisk Jem off on an adventure in the tropics, he'd promised to have him back in six months' time. It had taken them two months to cross the Atlantic, and they'd been living on Island X for two months now. So if everything went according to plan, Jem had very little time left before he'd have to trade the Lost Souls for his schoolmates, and tree house construction for Master Davis's long, droning lectures on prime numbers, Latin verbs, and character building. Back in the Old World, a rare adventure consisted of visiting his parents' estate, where the wildest animals around were a grumpy pony and a fat tabby cat.

Jem glanced around again. On the one hand, returning to a life of lessons and rules sounded terribly dull. On the other hand, at least his parents' tabby cat wouldn't eat him for breakfast.

He shook his head, and a lecture Master Davis had once given came to mind.

"Boys," the stuffy schoolmaster had declared, "the best way to overcome fear is to learn everything you can about whatever it is you're scared of. Logic conquers all."

That last bit didn't really apply to Island X, but Jem decided he'd give it a go anyway. If he was going to be a good Deputy Captain, he had to get over this fear. "Uncle Finn," he called, interrupting his uncle's lecture on the many exciting ways to phrase a hypothesis. "About that panther."

"Hmm?" Uncle Finn looked back over his shoulder. "What about it?"

Jem took a deep breath, wondering where to start.

"Well . . . what do panthers eat?"

"Meat," Uncle Finn said without hesitation. "They're carnivores."

"Right." Jem gulped. That hadn't helped. "And . . . how do you know when they're around?"

Uncle Finn paused to inspect a giant red bromeliad covered in tiny green ants. "You usually don't," he said. "Panthers are stealthy, almost completely silent. You don't know they're there until they're on top of you."

Jem's knees buckled. He silently cursed Master Davis.

"What about tracks?" Thomas asked, holding some vines to the side so they could pass.

"About this big." Uncle Finn held up his fist. "They have big round toe pads, but no claw marks. That's because their claws are retractable. They only unsheathe them when they want to kill something."

"Oh. Good," Jem wheezed, remembering the track Monty had shown him earlier that day. It had fit Uncle Finn's description perfectly. He looked around for a nice spot to lie down and pass out.

"I wonder if there are any other panthers on the island," Thomas mused. "Must get lonely in that cave all by 'imself. Bet he'd like a friend."

More than one panther? Jem had never thought about that. He wiped sweat off his forehead and looked behind him, this time spotting glimmering cat eyes in every bush. The jungle suddenly seemed darker. He scanned the treetops for a slice of sunlight.

All of a sudden, something came crashing through the bushes behind him. Jem whirled around just as the beast threw itself on him, landing square on his chest.

"Argh!" He stumbled backward. "Help! Get it off me!" He tripped over a fallen log and fell smack on his rear end, wrestling with the beast still clinging to his shirt.

"Easy there, Jem." Thomas leaned over and plucked the thing off him, holding up a small black monkey. The troublemaker shrieked with laughter. "It's jus' a little fella."

Jem let his breath out in a whoosh. It was just a monkey. Not a panther. He climbed slowly to his feet, dusting the dirt off his trousers and ignoring Uncle Finn's snicker. If he did have to return to the Old World, one thing he certainly wouldn't miss was the monkeys.

Actually, he realized as he glared at the jabbering little creature, it wasn't just any monkey. It was Kapu's pet monkey. Which meant the Islanders couldn't be far away. Which reminded him why he'd ventured out into the jungle in the first place.

Sure enough, a moment later, Sina and Kapu's tiny tree house came into view, and the pair emerged from it, swinging down on sturdy vines to greet their visitors. The monkey slipped out of Thomas's grasp and leaped onto Kapu's shoulder.

"Hey!" Jem called.

Kapu danced over to meet him with a big gap-toothed smile.

"You lost a tooth!" Jem exclaimed. Since Kapu knew even less English than Sina, Jem tapped his own tooth for emphasis. Kapu smiled wider and nodded.

"Where are you going?" Jem asked, miming the question by marching on the spot and lifting his palms up in question.

Sina pointed at Jem.

"To camp? That's great! Because I need your help." Jem pointed to himself, then tapped his head. "I need you to show me how to put a door on a tree house." He pointed up at their tree house, then mimed opening and shutting a door. Sina and Kapu had the most well-constructed house he'd ever seen. If anyone knew how to build a door, it was them.

Sina nodded, but she looked confused. She and Kapu had a short discussion, then turned back to Jem, mimed opening the door, and shrugged as if to say, "Why?"

"Well, to keep predators out," Jem explained. "Like the panther." He did his best imitation of a large bloodthirsty cat.

Sina looked amused. She said something to Kapu, who giggled.

Jem couldn't say for sure, but he had a feeling it was something along the lines of, "A door won't keep a panther out." And that was probably true, but he had to do something to protect the crew. This was the best he could come up with.

Sina raised a finger, then drew herself up tall, assuming an ugly grimace. Then she pretended to unsheathe a cutlass and brandish it in the air.

"Ooh!" Thomas exclaimed. "Pirates! Right? I like this game!"

"Come on, Thomas." Uncle Finn sighed, pulling his

assistant further into the jungle. "We'll see you children later," he called back to them.

"Oh, I see what you're saying," Jem said to Sina. "A door won't keep the pirates out, right?"

Sina shrugged.

Jem sighed. "True. It's . . . it's just all I've got for now. The Lucas problem is a much, much bigger one. To be honest, I'm hoping Scarlet will be back by the time we have to face it, so we can all put our heads together."

Sina studied him for a moment, then nodded. She hoisted her quiver of arrows and her bow up on her shoulder, then turned and headed for camp, motioning for the boys to fall in behind her.

They'd only been in the clearing for a minute or two when Smitty came running over, followed by Monty and Elmo.

"Fitz," he said seriously. "We've got a problem."

Jem froze. "What? What is it? *Who* is it?" Images of a Lost Soul getting carried away by a slobbering panther flashed through his mind. Or maybe Lucas had shown up already. What then? That would mean—

Smitty cleared his throat. "I have this . . . sickness."

Jem stopped. "You . . . what?" Smitty looked perfectly healthy.

"I have a sickness," Smitty repeated. "And I don't know what will cure it."

"Uh-huh." Jem raised an eyebrow.

"It's a love sickness," Smitty explained, and he

whipped a bouquet of half-wilted flowers out from behind his back. He presented them to Sina, who looked properly horrified.

Jem groaned as Monty and Elmo exploded into laughter. Kapu joined in, but Sina stopped him with a cuff upside the head.

"Isn't that sweet of Rodney?" cooed Elmo.

"Alfred, you shouldn't have!" Monty batted his eyelashes.

Jem sighed and rubbed his forehead. The Lost Souls were all trying extrahard to discover Smitty's real name now, hoping they'd make the right guess in front of Sina.

For her part, Sina didn't seem to appreciate the humor. Ignoring the wilted bouquet, she turned on her heel and stalked off.

"Wait!" Jem called, for he still needed her help with the doors. "Meet me at the houses, okay?" He nudged Kapu, who ran after his sister.

"You're welcome!" Smitty called. "See you later!"

Still howling with laughter, Monty and Elmo scampered off in the opposite direction.

Once they were gone, Jem gave Smitty a tired look, but the boy ignored him.

"Seriously, Fitz," he said. "I *do* have a problem."

"Sure you do, Smit. Look, I've got important things to do here, like fending off a panther that wants to eat us and a pirate who wants to make us clean the long drop for eternity. Or worse."

"This'll just take a minute. See, I need to show Sina how I feel about her."

"I think you've been doing just fine at that," Jem told him. "Now if you'll excuse me—"

"Please, Jem." Smitty took hold of his arm. "You're the smartest person I know. Help me think of a way to win her love?"

Jem threw up his hands. "I don't know anything about love!"

"Please, Jem." Smitty gave him a pitiful look.

Jem sighed. "Well . . . why don't you get Kapu to teach you the Islander language? That way you can actually talk to her. I'll bet she'd appreciate it." *And,* he added to himself, *it would be good to have someone other than Scarlet who can communicate with them.*

Smitty wrinkled his nose. "I was thinking something more along the lines of a poem."

"Of course you were."

"In fact, I just came up with one. Let me recite it, and you'll tell me what you think?"

"But Smit," said Jem, "what good is a poem if you don't speak the same language?"

"We speak the language of love!" Smitty answered.

Jem almost pointed out that Sina seemed to speak the language of "go away and leave me alone," then decided it would be faster not to argue. "Okay. But be quick."

"Jolly!" Smitty took a step back, then squared his shoulders and cleared his throat. "Ready?"

"You've got two minutes," Jem warned him.

"Okay." Smitty closed his eyes, then recited,

I'm just a simple pirate, a rotten buccaneer,
But something unexplicable hits me when
*   you are near.*

"Inexplicable," said Jem.

"Just listen, mate."

I've never felt this way before, I'm achy, sick,
*   and tired.*
I thought at first I'd eaten something after
*   it expired.*

Jem held up his hand. "Really?"

"Really," said Smitty. "This love thing is tearing me apart."

"No, I meant—" Jem began, then thought better. "Go on."

But then I realized it happens just when you're
*   around.*
My tongue goes numb, my mouth dries up,
*   I cannot make a sound.*

"So that's why it's been nice and quiet lately," Jem commented.

"Shh."

*It's not the pain I mind so much—that's not
what makes me blue.*

*It's wondering if you will ever say you love me,
too.*

Smitty sighed and bowed his head. "That's it."

"Good," Jem said, glad it was over.

"Think she'll like it?"

"I'm sure she will," Jem told him. "Although you might want to consider learning the Islander language, anyway. You know, in case this doesn't quite to do the job."

Smitty shrugged. "I'll try this first." And he trotted off, leaving Jem shaking his head.

CHAPTER SEVEN

Scarlet stared at the parlor ceiling and wondered if it was possible to die of boredom. If it was, she was probably dangerously close to her own demise.

In the stiff-backed chair beside her, Josephine hummed a little tune while working on her embroidery. She'd been at it for the last few hours, humming away as an orange cat took shape on her dainty white handkerchief.

"Would you say that you're a cat person, cousin?" Josephine asked, without looking up from her work.

"No," Scarlet replied, shaking her right leg, which had fallen asleep around the same time her brain went numb, a good two hours before.

"Well, I definitely am," said Josephine. "I just adore cats. Big ones, small ones, striped ones—"

"Right. I figured," Scarlet cut in. Josephine's favorite topics, as she'd discovered over the past few days, were embroidery, knitting, and cats. The cousins officially had nothing in common.

Death by boredom. Scarlet shifted in her stiff-backed chair and shook her head in disgust. *What a horrible way to go.* Death by keelhaul would be honorable. Death by plank-walking would be brave. Even death by snakebite would be understandable. But no one would understand if they found the captain of the Lost Souls dead in a King's Man's parlor with a mess of embroidery in her lap.

She looked down at her own project and grimaced. The yellow butterfly she'd envisioned flitting across the handkerchief looked more like an egg someone had dropped on the road.

Josephine glanced up. "Do you need some help, cousin?"

"No," said Scarlet. "I'm going to take a break." She stood, stretching her restless legs. "Hard work, this embroidery."

Josephine gave her an encouraging smile. "It's coming along well." She looked down at the yellow splat and bit her lip. "I can't believe embroidery isn't taught in the tropics."

"Yes, we're really missing out." Scarlet tossed the handkerchief aside and marched to the window. The ocean view had an instant calming effect, and she reminded herself to be nice.

"Here in the tropics, ladies are really more into . . ." She racked her brain for something a lady would do. "Spices," she said. It wasn't entirely a lie—the Islander women had known all about spices. They'd spent hours gathering and drying and grinding them into fine powders, then sharing them with family and friends. Some simply tasted delicious, like the cinnamon Meggie sprinkled on Scarlet's toast every morning now. Other spices had different powers—healing powers, or so Scarlet's mother had told her, so long ago.

"Spices!" Josephine dropped her embroidery in her lap. "Really?"

"Mm-hm." Scarlet looked away, gazing out the

window at the milky-blue sea in the distance.

"Like the Islanders used to use!" said Josephine. "Father was telling me all about them," she added. "They sounded like fascinating people. I mean, can you imagine living in a little hut made of wood and leaves, and going around barefoot? I just—" Suddenly, Josephine stopped. "Oh, cousin, I'm sorry. I completely forgot you were . . . I mean, you are . . ."

Scarlet kept staring out the window, hoping Josephine would take the hint and drop the subject. She could just imagine what Uncle Daniel had said about the Islanders—the people he hadn't wanted his brother to live with. Her hands balled into fists.

She focused on the horizon to calm herself. Somewhere out there was her island, and on it, her crew. What were they up to now? Had Jem managed to fend off the panther? Had there been any sign of the power-hungry pirate captain?

"Maybe . . . maybe you can show me how the Islanders used spices," Josephine suggested. "I'm sure my schoolmistress will be fascinated when I report back."

"Maybe," Scarlet answered, knowing full well she would do no such thing.

"My father is particularly fascinated by the Islanders," Josephine went on, and Scarlet rolled her eyes. "And particularly their knowledge of plants that cure illnesses. Like—"

"Why don't we go outside?" Scarlet interrupted. Her legs and lungs ached for a walk and some fresh air.

And it would give her a chance to eavesdrop on some conversations around port and maybe learn a thing or two about the Rebel.

"Oh." Josephine's eyes grew wide. "But our fathers won't be home for another hour at least, remember?"

Scarlet's father and Uncle Daniel had left that morning to consult with some other King's Men about Uncle Daniel's business, which Scarlet still couldn't define. She'd asked him about it, but he'd droned on so long about the king's greatness and how lucky he was to work for him that she'd eventually stopped listening.

"That's all right," said Scarlet. "We'll be back before they are."

"B-but . . . without a chaperone?" Josephine clutched her handkerchief with both hands.

"Sure," Scarlet said, although she could picture her father exploding if he saw them out alone. "That's . . . that's how it's done in the tropics." It was a full-out lie, but possibly the only way to get Josephine outside of the house and away from her embroidery.

"Really?" Josephine looked uncertain.

"Definitely," Scarlet told her. "Chaperones are an Old World thing. Here in the tropics, they don't even exist. Come on now." She strode to the parlor door and waited for Josephine to rise and join her.

"Should we tell Meggie?"

"No," Scarlet said quickly. "She won't care. Come on. I'll show you around. Then you can report back to your classmates about the *real* tropics."

Josephine practically glued herself to Scarlet's side as they wandered down the muddy red street, away from the admiral's house and toward the docks. She took everything in without blinking, gasping when an old merchant offered to sell them limes, and squeaking when a cabin boy ran by, splashing their boots with red mud.

"Watch where you're going!" Scarlet yelled after him, and Josephine gasped again.

"We're not allowed to raise our voices in public back in the Old World," she murmured. "Or anywhere, really."

"Oh. Right." Scarlet pictured her father reminding her of Rule Number Five. Good thing he hadn't been around for that. "Come on." She dragged Josephine across the street, away from some filthy pirates who were eyeing them curiously. Children didn't get noticed in port when they were dressed up like cabin boys, but apparently unchaperoned girls in fine dresses did. Scarlet suddenly remembered how Jem and his uncle had been greeted when they'd first stepped off their ship, dressed all posh and proper. The *Dark Ranger* pirates had lost no time in kidnapping them and hauling them onto their own boat.

She glanced behind her at the pirates, silently cursing her stiff new boots, which were too tight to house her dagger. "Let's hurry," she said, pulling Josephine toward the docks.

Once the sparkling ocean lay before them, she

began to breathe easier. Even Josephine relaxed her grip on Scarlet's arm as she took in all the ships anchored in the bay.

"Are . . . are any of these . . . *pirate* ships?" she whispered. "Do those really exist?"

Scarlet stifled a laugh. "They do exist," she told her cousin. "In fact, you're surrounded by them."

Josephine looked around, mouth open, as a grizzled old sea dog stomped by. "No one back home will ever believe it," she whispered, and Scarlet had to smile, having heard Jem say the same thing many times. The two of them would probably get along just fine.

"Look, there's a whole group of them." Josephine pointed off to the right, and Scarlet turned to look. Sure enough, a crowd of pirates was huddled some ten yards away, listening to something or someone in the middle of their circle. A few jostled for a better view.

"Hmm." Scarlet watched them for a moment. Something was definitely up. "Come on." She pulled Josephine closer to the crowd.

"Oh, but—" her cousin began to protest.

"Shh." Scarlet stopped a few feet outside the circle and leaned in, listening hard.

"And what's in it for us?" one pirate yelled.

"Whatever you want," came the answer from inside the huddle. "Money, jewels, slaves. Whatever you dream of."

The crowd murmured. Josephine opened her mouth to speak, but Scarlet raised a finger to her lips. That voice was familiar . . .

"They say ye can wrestle a smelly wild pig," another pirate shouted. "That true?"

"With one hand tied behind my back," came the reply.

Now it was Scarlet's turn to gasp. It was Lucas Lawrence. She'd know a boast coming out of his big mouth anywhere.

"What's the matter?" Josephine whispered, but Scarlet shook her head. Lucas sounded like he was recruiting new men. For the *Dark Ranger*, maybe? Or . . .

"Blimey!"

"Cousin!" Josephine whispered, shocked.

But Scarlet waved her off. *No,* she told herself. *That's not possible.*

"Look!" someone yelled. And the entire crowd turned at once to look in Scarlet's and Josephine's direction. Scarlet grabbed her cousin's arm, dragging her to one side of the dock. But the crowd of pirates didn't even notice them. They were looking past the girls, at two men who'd just appeared at the end of the dock, looking like the sea had just spewed them up. Their shirts and trousers were barely more than rags, and their skin was so sunburned it hurt to look at it. One wore a filthy bandana around his head, and the other had made a hat out of seaweed to protect himself from the sun.

"Sink me," Scarlet whispered.

"What?" Josephine asked. "Who's that?"

"You've got to be joking . . ."

For a moment, the pirates stared, wide-eyed, at the Dread Pirate Captain Wallace Hammerstein-Jones and his right-hand man, Iron "Pete" Morgan. Then suddenly, all together, they began to chortle. The chortling soon escalated into guffaws, then hoots of laughter.

Lucas Lawrence stepped out of the circle, meaty hands on his hips, and drew himself up tall. "Wallace!" he shouted. "You're here!"

He didn't call him "Captain," Scarlet thought, feeling dizzy. *Does it mean what I think it means? Scurvy, what if—*

"You . . . you . . . ," Captain Wallace sputtered, staggering forward on feet that obviously hadn't touched firm ground in weeks. "You *scalawag*!"

Lucas laughed, and the men echoed him.

"You traitor!" Captain Wallace continued, staggering closer. "You think you can cross me? You think you can steal my men and my ship and get away with it?"

Lucas folded his arms across his chest. "Looks like I did."

Captain Wallace looked like he could breathe fire. "You think you've got what it takes to take over the tropics? You? A mere . . . *child*!"

"Blast!" Scarlet whispered. *Lucas* was the Rebel. "Bilge and blimey!"

"Cousin!" Josephine gasped.

Lucas narrowed his eyes at Captain Wallace. "Just watch me, *Wallace*."

Captain Wallace let out a strangled cry and stumbled forward, but two enormous pirates stepped out and blocked his way. A cloud of curses filled the air, and the pirates began to shift and surge.

Scarlet shook herself out of her stupor and grabbed her cousin's hand. "Come on," she said, pulling Josephine away from the rowdy crowd. "We should go home."

"Well," Josephine said as they walked back. "That was certainly . . . interesting." She reached into a pocket and drew out her pink fan, fluttering it in front of her face.

Scarlet took several deep breaths, trying to get the hurricane of thoughts in her head under control. Lucas had mutinied against Captain Wallace. And now he was bent on being the most powerful captain in the tropics. Part of her wanted to pull out her hair, while a larger part wanted to run back to the docks and pull out his.

Did the crew know about this? With so many miles between them, who could say? But until she could be back with them, she had to do what she'd promised: find out more about the Rebel's—Lucas's—plan.

Not to mention Captain Wallace's plan for revenge.

CHAPTER EIGHT

"Hold it still," Jem called, giving the nail a final whack with his hammer. "There!" He stepped back to admire his handiwork. "Not bad, right?"

Kapu tested the door, swinging it back and forth. He nodded.

"Come on, it's good, isn't it?" Jem tested the door himself. "It'll keep out the panther." He turned to the younger boy and bared his teeth—an expression that had become their sign for "panther."

Kapu looked at the door, then gave Jem a look that said, "If you say so."

Jem frowned. They'd been at this door for two hours and still had three more to install. "What's wrong with it?"

Kapu got down on all fours. Obviously pretending to be a panther, he skulked toward the door, gave it a sniff, then lowered his shoulder and shoved it, hard. The door swung right open, and Kapu turned to Jem with a look that said, "See?"

Jem bit his lip. "All right, so we'll put a lock on it. We'll secure it."

Kapu raised his right hand and curled his fingers, as if showing off some sharp claws.

"Oh." Jem sighed. "You think he can tear right through it. I didn't think of that." He set his hammer down on the tree house floor and folded his arms across his chest. "Well then, do you have any better ideas?" He tapped his head.

Kapu rocked back on his feet and thought for a moment. Then he snapped his fingers.

"You've got something? What?"

Kapu got back on all fours, pretending once again to be the panther, skulking through the jungle. Then suddenly, he let out a howl and flipped onto his side.

"What?" Jem cried. "What happened?"

Kapu pointed to his foot, which he kept glued to the floor while flailing all his other limbs.

"Oh! A trap!" Jem exclaimed, pausing to congratulate himself on how good he was getting at communicating with the Islanders.

Kapu sprang to his feet, nodding.

"Right. We can't do that." Jem shook his head. "Ronagh would slay us all." He swiped his hand across his throat.

Now Kapu's shoulders sagged.

"But good idea," said Jem. "Got anything else?"

They swung down to the jungle floor and surveyed the situation. Jem still couldn't help thinking that the doors weren't altogether useless. At least they'd give the panther some kind of obstacle in his path toward dinner. He shuddered at the thought. "What about—"

"Jem! Jem!"

Jem whirled around. "What on earth?"

"*Jeeeeem!*" Ronagh came tearing across the clearing, her face the color of an extraripe grapefruit.

"Now, stop right there!" Uncle Finn was hot on her heels, his own face shiny with sweat.

"What the flotsam?" Jem cried as the hefty explorer and the tiny girl slid to a stop in front of him.

"Your uncle is being *horrible*!" Ronagh shrieked. "You've got to—"

"Don't listen to her," Uncle Finn huffed. "She just—"

"You *are* horrible! You're—"

"STOP!" Jem bellowed, once again feeling like he'd channeled Scarlet. "What's going on? Ronagh, you start."

Ronagh gave Uncle Finn a poisonous look. "Uncle Finn is . . . is *experimenting*."

Jem and Kapu exchanged a glance. "Experimenting?" Jem repeated.

Ronagh nodded. "The scoundrel."

Jem crouched down and put a hand on the girl's shoulder. "Ro, you know he's a scientist, right? That's what he does."

"I *know*." Ronagh shrugged his hand away. "That's the problem."

Jem stood back up. "I think you need to explain some more."

"I'll explain," Uncle Finn cut in. "I *have* been experimenting. And with great effect! Nine of the last ten samples I tested produced a full head of hair on a specimen lacking one! This is it, my boy! The experiment is—"

Ronagh shrieked and lunged for Uncle Finn.

"Ro!" Jem caught her by the arm before she could pummel his uncle.

"And *you* are making a big deal over nothing!" Uncle Finn cried, stepping out of Ronagh's way. "I thought your vegetarianism was crazy, but *this*!"

By now, a few other Lost Souls had gathered to watch.

"Jem!" Ronagh yanked her arm away. "He's using the animals! For *science*!"

Jem looked up at his uncle. "You're what?"

"Just a few tests," Uncle Finn huffed. "Nothing that will harm them long-term. You see, I ran out of humans to test my plant samples on. *I've* already got a full head of hair." He tossed it for effect. "As does Thomas."

"So he's using the monkeys!" Ronagh yelled. "He's feeding them plants and making them all . . . *hairy*!" She lunged again for Uncle Finn, this time slipping past Jem.

"Which means it's working! Ow!" Uncle Finn cried as she pounded his stomach with her small fists. "They don't mind a little more hair. Who wouldn't want more hair?"

"Look!" Ronagh stopped pounding and grabbed Jem by the wrist, pulling him over to a tree. Uncle Finn and the Lost Souls who'd stopped to watch followed. "There!" Ronagh pointed high up into the branches. "See?"

Jem squinted. "Where?"

Ronagh whistled, and a few seconds later, a small black monkey came swinging down to see her.

Except he couldn't see her, with all the hair in his eyes. He vaulted off a branch, but instead of landing on Ronagh's shoulder, he crashed right into the dirt. Ronagh rushed over and pulled him up, pushing his hair out of his face. It promptly fell back over his eyes.

"See?" Ronagh yelled. *"See?"*

Jem groaned. "Uncle Finn! You can't do that. It's wrong."

"No," Uncle Finn replied, "it's *science*. Look at the hair on that creature! It's beautiful!"

Jem smacked his forehead.

"And who else am I supposed to test on?" Uncle Finn looked around at the Lost Souls. Several ducked and covered their heads.

"How about some pirates in port?" Elmo suggested. "Lots of them could use some more hair."

"Yeah," said Charlie. "Go to port and feed 'em your plants, then go back a few days later and check up on 'em."

That, Jem had to admit, was a pretty good idea. Even Ronagh looked somewhat appeased as she began braiding the monkey's hair away from his face.

Uncle Finn twirled a lock of hair around his finger. "You think I should go to port?"

"Yes." Jem sighed. "You should. Go test your plants on the pirates." *Maybe that will keep them away from Island X for a while longer,* he thought. He suddenly felt very, very tired.

"Hmph." Uncle Finn tossed his hair over his shoulder. "Well, all right then. From now on, I'll test on pirates. Happy?" he asked Ronagh, who ignored him.

Uncle Finn marched back to the clearing, and the other Lost Souls began to wander off, leaving Jem and Kapu alone again.

"If only all problems could resolve themselves so easily," Jem said.

Kapu nodded and bared his teeth.

"Right, like the panther." Jem sighed.

Kapu pretended to unsheathe a cutlass and wave it around.

"And Lucas." Jem sighed again. "Don't remind me. If only there were some way to protect ourselves from both at once." He leaned back to look up at the trees, as if the answer might fall down from them into his lap.

Kapu yelped and tugged on Jem's sleeve.

"What?" Jem looked back down, into the boy's excited eyes. "You have an idea?"

Kapu nodded, throwing himself down on all fours again. He began to crawl across the jungle floor, then made a big show of stepping on something with his right hand.

"Another trap?" Jem asked. "I don't think—"

Kapu shook his head and raised a finger. Then he went back to being the panther, stepping on something with his right hand. Suddenly, he sprang to his feet. *"Crash! Clang! Aaaa!"* he yelled.

Jem jumped back. For a moment he wondered if Kapu had gone off the deep end. Then it occurred to him. "A trap that sets off noise!" he cried. "A trap that doesn't hurt the panther, but scares it off and wakes everyone up!"

Kapu nodded, dancing a joyful jig.

"I like it!" Jem jabbed a finger in the air. "Good thinking."

Kapu took a small bow, then ran off into the trees.

"This is great!" Jem said, heading back to the center

of the clearing, where he'd left most of his tools. "A noisemaker trap. We'll need some rope. And wire. And maybe some tin plates from the *Hop*? And . . . and hollow sticks that knock together." The possibilities for noisemakers were endless.

About fifteen minutes later, Kapu appeared, holding three small gourds, which must have come from Sina's garden. He held a finger up to his lips and wiggled his eyebrows as if to say, "Don't tell." Then he grabbed Jem's knife, cut the top off one, and proceeded to hollow it out.

"Oh, I see," said Jem. "You're going to make a big rattle. Will you fill it with rocks? Or seeds?"

Kapu nodded, concentrating on his handiwork. Jem grabbed another gourd and followed his lead.

They worked for over an hour, constructing all the noisemakers they could think of, while Jem praised Kapu's idea at least a half dozen more times.

"If this works, maybe we can make more than one of these traps," he mused. "And what do you think of—"

"*Jeeeeem!*"

"Not again!" Jem dropped his gourd and turned to see Tim running toward him, his face roughly the same grapefruit color as Ronagh's had been. "What *now*?"

"It's Uncle Finn!" Tim yelled, skidding to a stop near their workstation.

"Swig, it's okay," Jem said. "It's all been solved. He and Thomas are going to go to port and—"

"Exactly!" Tim wrung his hands. "He *went* to port!"

"So? What's wrong with that? I thought it was a good idea."

"You *told* him and Thomas to go?"

"Well . . . yes." Jem stared up at the quartermaster. "What on earth is the matter, Swig?"

"I'll tell you what's the matter!" Tim pulled at his dirty hair with both hands. "They took the *Hop*!"

CHAPTER NINE

"Can you imagine, Josephine, how impressed your schoolmates will be when you tell them about your trip?" Uncle Daniel said as they strolled through Port Aberhard toward the docks. "The tropics are just so fascinating. So . . ." He took a deep breath of the humid air. "So full of *possibilities.*"

Josephine *hmm*ed politely, lifting her skirt a few inches off the ground as she tiptoed over a mud puddle.

Scarlet stepped right into it without noticing, preoccupied by all the pirates around her. *Which ones were Lucas's crewmates?* she wondered. *Had he told any of them about the treasure on Island X, or was he keeping that secret to himself for now? Surely—*

"Scarlet?"

"Hmm?" She shook herself back to the present. Uncle Daniel and Josephine were both staring at her feet. She looked down to find herself ankle-deep in red mud.

"Oh. Oops." She sloshed out and continued walking.

"I'm particularly intrigued by all that . . . vegetation." Uncle Daniel waved at the jungle that leaned right up against the port town, almost as if it wanted to push the whole thing out to sea. "Think how many plants in there have undiscovered powers. It's mind-boggling."

He should meet Uncle Finn, Scarlet thought, then quickly dismissed it. That would involve going to Island

X, and there was no way she was bringing her Old World uncle to her home.

"It is fascinating," Josephine agreed. "Just . . . a bit hot."

Uncle Daniel's eyes snapped down to her. "Are you feeling unwell, dear?" He reached for her hand.

"Oh no, I'm fine. It's just—"

"You look flushed." Uncle Daniel peered into her face. "Perhaps we should go back to the house so you can lie down."

"Oh no, I'm—" Josephine began to protest.

But Uncle Daniel tucked her hand into the crook of his arm. "Scarlet, dear, would you guide us home? Josephine is unwell."

Scarlet looked from her cousin to her uncle and back again. Josephine didn't look any less well than usual. In fact, she looked better now than she had when she'd arrived a few days ago. Her cheeks were flushed, but it *was* the middle of the afternoon, and no one in their right mind went for a stroll in the middle of the afternoon in the tropics. Well, except an Old Worlder who didn't know any better.

Still, she steered them back to her father's house without argument, watching out of the corner of her eye as Uncle Daniel escorted her cousin down the street, bent over her as if sheltering her from a gale.

Well, she thought as they reached the house, *at least my father doesn't do that.* Uncle Daniel made the admiral's father-daughter meetings seem downright reasonable.

Admiral McCray himself met them at the front door. He took one look at his brother and Josephine and rushed forward.

"I'm fine," Josephine said quickly.

"She wasn't feeling well," Uncle Daniel explained. "Shall we sit down in the parlor?"

"Of course!" The admiral ushered them inside.

"Well," he said, once Josephine was stretched out on a sofa in the parlor and Meggie had been dispatched for tea. "I was going to suggest we dine at Humphries's tonight, but if Josephine's unwell, I'll just tell him—"

"Oh, please don't." Josephine sat up. "I'm fine, really. I was a bit warm, that's all. Father, you've been so looking forward to dinner with Humphries."

"True," said Uncle Daniel, "I haven't seen Humphries in ages. But your health is far more—"

"I'm well," Josephine cut in. "Truly."

Scarlet raised her eyebrows. She wasn't entirely certain, but something told her that proper ladies didn't interrupt their fathers. Actually, it might have been her own father who'd told her that. It might have been Rule Number Fourteen or whatever number they were on.

"Who's Humphries?" she asked as Meggie marched in with a tray of tea and biscuits.

"A good friend from the Old World," Uncle Daniel answered, helping Josephine off the sofa and over to the table. "He left years ago to start a plantation here. Apparently it's a very lucrative business, or so he says in his letters."

"Oh." Scarlet's stomach twisted at the word

plantation. She stole a glance at her father, hoping to catch his eye and give him a desperate "you're not going to make *me* go there, are you?" look. But he wouldn't look at her.

"I still find it hard to imagine," Uncle Daniel went on, "how Humphries could give up his life in a bustling city, ship a few trunkloads of belongings halfway around the world, and set up a new life where civilization barely exists!" He shook his head and dumped three big spoonfuls of sugar in his teacup. "But I'm eager to learn about plantations here in the tropics."

"It's a very big and fancy house," Josephine told Scarlet. "We'll have to wear all our finest. Isn't that exciting?"

"I can barely contain myself," Scarlet replied, gulping down her tea.

She could feel her father's eyes on her, giving her a warning look. But this time, she didn't look at him.

"This is so exciting," Josephine chattered as she braided her hair. "I've never seen a real plantation before. What do you think it will be like?"

Scarlet sat on her bed, trying to muster the will to change into the sky-blue dress that had somehow appeared in her closet while she and Josephine and Uncle Daniel had been out walking that afternoon. Its frills and poufs and ribbons had practically made her lose her lunch. What had she ever done to Meggie for the maid to have it out for her this way?

"I can tell you what it'll be like," she said, tucking her legs up under her and closing her eyes. "Picture a jungle. A great big beautiful tangle of trees and vines and ferns and flowers like you've never seen before." She closed her eyes, imagining her home. "And in that jungle live thousands of animals. There are butterflies of every color imaginable. Birds that squawk and birds that sing sweetly. Huge lizards that can walk upside down on the branches, but never fall off, not even when you'd bet your life they will. And there are monkeys, too. They crash through the treetops, swinging from their tails while their babies hold on tight to their backs."

She opened her eyes to find Josephine standing still, her fingers frozen in her half-braided hair and her eyes fixed on Scarlet. "And?" she whispered.

"And that's what was there before the plantation," Scarlet finished flatly. "Now it's just row after row of sugarcane." She stood up and walked to the closet—not because she wanted to see the dress, but because she suspected if she kept talking about the jungle, she'd lose it completely. She'd once sworn never to set foot on a plantation, and here she was, going to dine at a most . . . what was the word her uncle had used? A most *lucrative* one. And in the most hideous dress in existence. A strangled whimper escaped her before she could stop it.

"Here." Josephine finished her braiding and came to stand behind Scarlet. "I'll help you." She began to untie Scarlet's ribbons.

"I don't need . . . ," Scarlet began, then gave up. Realistically, the only way she was going to get dressed and out the door was with someone's help. Meggie obviously hated the job, especially after Scarlet had accidentally kicked her in the shin while trying to get into a hideous green frock. So Josephine would have to do. "We don't . . . wear clothes like this . . . at my school . . . so . . . ," she explained feebly.

Josephine just hummed in response.

Somehow, within fifteen minutes, Scarlet was not only dressed but her hair was braided like her cousin's, pulled back from her face so it didn't keep falling in her eyes.

"How's that?" Josephine stepped back to admire her handiwork.

Scarlet patted her head and had to admit it wasn't bad. In fact, it was almost as good as wearing a hat.

Josephine pulled on her boots and laced them up, and Scarlet watched her, allowing herself for a moment to imagine what life would have been like if she hadn't run away to become a pirate, and had gone instead to live in the Old World with Josephine. Would they have been like sisters? Would Scarlet have been sent to finishing school, too? Would she have ever survived?

But there was no time to ponder it, for the admiral was calling for them. Josephine gave Scarlet a once-over, then took her hand and pulled her out the door.

The carriage bounced down the plantation road, lined on either side by endless rows of leafy sugarcane plants twice Scarlet's height.

"Isn't this amazing?" Uncle Daniel said, half leaning out the side. "What an empire Humphries has made! Look how these plants prosper here. Row upon row upon row of them!"

"The jungle that was here in the first place was pretty prosperous, too," Scarlet pointed out, and received an elbow in the ribs from her father. "Well, it's true," she murmured.

"It's enormous," Uncle Daniel marveled. "He must have dozens of workers out there."

Josephine peered out at the sugarcane. "Did he bring them from the Old World?" she asked.

Uncle Daniel shook his head. "No need for that. Inexpensive labor is easy to find here."

Admiral McCray frowned. "Inexpensive, but not free, I hope."

Uncle Daniel shrugged, still peering out the window. "I'm not sure. He hasn't mentioned anything about . . . about that in his letters. But I understand it's not uncommon."

"What's not uncommon?" Scarlet asked.

"Slavery," said Admiral McCray. "Employing laborers but not paying them."

"Oh, I'm sure a friend of Father's wouldn't do that," said Josephine. "Right, Father?"

"Well, I don't know," said Uncle Daniel. "I'd hope not, but plantations do require an enormous workload, for planting and—"

"That's no excuse for holding people captive," the admiral said coldly.

Scarlet's head swiveled from her father to her uncle and back. She hadn't even considered that plantations might use slaves as laborers. Just when she thought they couldn't get any worse!

She'd just opened her mouth to suggest they turn around and head home when the sugarcane suddenly fell away, revealing an enormous white house with white trim and white pillars.

"Ohhh," Josephine breathed. "It's beautiful!"

"Just what I expected!" said Uncle Daniel.

Scarlet squinted and shaded her eyes. "It's blinding," she said. "Who needs a house that big? It's—" Her father elbowed her again, and she gritted her teeth and clammed up.

As soon as the carriage stopped in front of the big white house, the front door swung open, and a tall, thin man with a shiny bald head stepped out to greet them. He was dressed in loose white linen, and his skin had been darkened and wrinkled by the sun. Another man followed, wearing a black suit complete with bow tie and white gloves.

"Humphries!" Uncle Daniel hopped out of the carriage and bounded up the steps to meet his old friend. The two men embraced while the other man helped the girls out of the carriage.

"Come in, come in, all of you." Humphries ushered them up the steps and through the front door. "My wife and daughter are so excited to meet you." He turned to the man in the black suit. "Fetch Mrs. Humphries and Cecily." The man bowed and disappeared inside.

"Who's that man?" Scarlet whispered to Josephine.

"Why, the butler, of course," Josephine whispered back. "You know, the one who answers doors and fetches things," she added when Scarlet looked blank.

"Oh. Right. Of course," said Scarlet, although she'd never heard of a butler before. Judging by the man's unsmiling face, it couldn't have been a very fun job.

They stopped in the main foyer, which was even grander than the one in the admiral's house. The chandelier was twice as big, and the floors and banisters gleamed so brightly that Scarlet could see her reflection in them. The white ceiling was as high as one of the aras' nesting trees. It made Scarlet feel small in a way the jungle never did. Out there, she was another creature, with a purpose and a role to play. Here she just felt out of place.

"Ah, here they are," Humphries said, as a woman in a dark red dress strode in, followed by a younger woman in a green dress who looked about five years older than Scarlet. Both had shiny brown curls that bounced as they walked, and Scarlet's hand immediately crept up to her own hair, still tightly braided. Then she shook her head and dropped her hand. Not that she gave a fig about hair.

"Time for introductions," said Humphries.

"Of course," said Uncle Daniel. "You remember my brother, Admiral John McCray?"

"I believe we met once or twice." The admiral offered his hand.

"Ages ago," Humphries agreed. "In another world."

"This is my daughter, Josephine, and John's daughter, Scarlet," Uncle Daniel said.

Scarlet concentrated hard on staying upright as she gripped her skirt and curtsied. She wobbled fiercely, but managed, miraculously, not to fall on her face.

"And this is my wife, Mrs. June Humphries, and our daughter, Cecily," said Humphries.

Scarlet watched as Cecily executed a perfect curtsy, curls bouncing politely. She had a heart-shaped face, a blush of pink across her cheeks, and pale, creamy skin like Josephine's. But there was something familiar about her. Scarlet was sure she'd seen her somewhere before—maybe in port? Maybe she'd even stolen something from her? She was racking her brain, trying to remember, when Cecily looked over and caught her staring. She narrowed her eyes and looked Scarlet up and down, and Scarlet reddened under her gaze. She didn't know Cecily one bit, but she was certain they'd never be friends.

Somewhere deep inside the house, a door slammed, and footsteps came running toward them.

"And there's our boy." Humphries sighed. "Always fashionably late."

The boy burst into the foyer, breathless and red-faced, his brown hair damp with sweat. "I'm sorry, everyone," he said. "I was out supervising the new crew. Couldn't quite make it back from the fields in time."

Scarlet's mouth fell open.

The boy straightened his coat, then bowed to Uncle Daniel and her father. "I'm Ben Hodgins."

"Shivers!" The word escaped Scarlet's mouth before she could stop it. She slapped a hand over her mouth, feeling her father's incredulous eyes on her.

Ben Hodgins turned to look at her, and his lower lip went slack.

"What was that, Scarlet?" asked Humphries.

"Oh." Scarlet tore her wide eyes away from Ben's, only to find that everyone in the room was staring at her. Her ears grew hot. "Oh. I'm sorry. I just . . . got cold. Suddenly." She shivered for effect and looked down at the gleaming floor, willing it to split open and swallow her. For somehow, *somehow*, she'd ended up in the same house as Ben Hodgins, the former captain of the Lost Souls. The one who'd taken her in when she ran away from home, and then made her captain when he left.

Because he'd fallen in love with a plantation owner's daughter, Scarlet remembered. *That* was why she recognized Cecily—she'd seen her with Ben in port one day not so long ago.

"Do you two know each other?" asked Humphries. His shiny forehead wrinkled.

"No!" Scarlet and Ben said in unison.

"Of course not," added Ben. He smoothed down his flyaway hair and stepped up to shake her father's and uncle's hands.

"Why would we?" added Scarlet. She wiped her sweaty hands on her dress, then remembered Rule Number One and tucked them behind her back.

Well, this was a fine mess. Here she was, on a horrible plantation with her former captain and dressed head to toe in ridiculous blue frills. It couldn't get any worse than this, she was certain.

"Ben is the best plantation manager I've ever had," Humphries boasted. "He and Cecily will be married in . . . how long now?"

"Less than a month," his wife said.

"Is it that soon?" Humphries looked at Cecily. She nodded, curls bouncing excitedly.

"Congratulations," offered Admiral McCray, and Daniel and Josephine echoed him.

"Congratulations," Scarlet muttered, although she couldn't imagine what Ben had been thinking, falling in love with a thing like Cecily.

Thankfully, the butler arrived then to let them know that dinner was served, and Humphries ushered them off to the dining hall.

Scarlet hung back, and Ben did the same, but before they could say a word, Cecily turned around and beckoned Ben with her finger.

"Right. Coming," he said, hurrying to catch up with her.

"Right," Scarlet said. "Coming." She waited a moment longer, to see if the floor might still split open and swallow her.

When it didn't, she gave in and followed.

The table was enormous, draped with a spotless white cloth, set with white dinner plates, and decorated with white flowers. Scarlet took her seat, certain she was going to spill something. Something red. Something that could never be removed.

Don't think. Just do, she told herself, remembering Jem's advice. *Just act like everything's normal. It'll all be over soon.*

Unfortunately, Ben took a seat right across from her, and Cecily took the one beside him. "What a lovely party we'll be," she remarked.

"Lovely," Josephine agreed, slipping into the chair next to Scarlet.

Don't think. Just do.

When the first course arrived (a rich red soup, of course), Scarlet went to pick up her spoon, only to find that there were not one, not two, but *three* spoons laid out before her, each a slightly different size. She looked around, wondering if the servants had made a mistake and given her *everyone's* spoon. But no, every single place had three.

Blimey, she thought. After studying each one, she picked up the medium-size spoon.

A bony elbow landed in her ribs, and she stole a glance at Josephine, who looked as if Scarlet had unknowingly picked up a snake.

All right, then. Scarlet dropped the medium-size spoon and moved her hand toward the small one, but Josephine shook her head. That obviously wasn't right, either. Scarlet pulled back, hand hovering over the large one, and Josephine relaxed.

Scarlet picked up the large spoon, making a mental note to explain to her cousin that in the tropics, spoons usually only came in one size.

"Josephine, my father tells me you attend a fine

finishing school back in the Old World," Cecily spoke up. "And Scarlet, you're at boarding school here in the tropics?"

Scarlet nodded, then realized that there couldn't be *that* many schools in the tropics. Cecily might well have gone to one. "Um, yes. Did you?"

Cecily shook her head. "I completed my schooling back in the Old World, then joined my mother and father here once I was finished."

Scarlet sighed with relief. "Oh. That's good. I mean . . . you must have . . . a good education." She sunk her spoon in her soup, concentrating hard on not spilling.

Cecily nodded. "Schools in the Old World are far superior. They teach *real* manners."

Scarlet paused with her spoon halfway to her mouth. Had Cecily just insulted her?

Ben cleared his throat. "Do you have a favorite class, Josephine?" he asked.

"Etiquette," Josephine replied, dabbing the corner of her mouth with a cloth. "It's just *so* important."

Cecily nodded. "I agree. I don't suppose they teach etiquette at your school, Scarlet?"

Scarlet set her spoon down, bristling on behalf of her nonexistent school. *Why, you lily-livered* . . . she thought, then replied, too sweetly, "Of course we do. But we also know it's not the only course that matters."

"How fascinating it must be," Josephine cut in, her voice a bit too loud. "To live on a plantation. We were discussing it in the carriage. It just sounds . . . very interesting," she finished, giving Scarlet a nervous glance.

"That's right," said Scarlet, staring Cecily square in the eye. "We were wondering about your laborers. Maybe you could explain how that works. We're just so . . . *ignorant*." She silently thanked Jem for arming her with a few big words.

Scarlet's father shot her a look, but oddly, the anger in it didn't seem directed at her.

Across from her, Ben's face clouded over, and he stared hard at his soup.

"Well," Humphries harrumphed from down the table. "That's hardly a topic for young ladies to discuss."

There was an awkward pause, then Cecily spoke up again. "Oh, excuse poor Scarlet, Father," she said, her lips pressed into a tight, vengeful line. "She goes to an island school where they aren't taught real manners."

"You little—" Scarlet began.

"Miss Scarlet!" Ben cried, then lowered his voice. "Y-you were about to tell us about your favorite class at school." His eyes pleaded her to say something that made sense.

"Oh, that's right." Cecily smiled. "Pray tell, what is it, Scarlet?"

"Well." Scarlet cleared her throat and tried hard to remember classes that Jem had mentioned taking. "I do enjoy . . . cartology."

She heard her father sigh.

"Cartology?" Cecily repeated. "Don't you mean *cartography*? The study of maps?"

Blast. "No," Scarlet said. "I mean *cartology*. The study of . . . carts."

"Scarlet's school," Admiral McCray spoke up, "focuses on . . . transportation."

"Really?" Mrs. Humphries asked, looking at Scarlet as if she'd just noticed her third eye.

"Really?" Cecily's curls bounced suspiciously. Scarlet imagined how satisfying it would be to snip them right off, one at a time.

"That sounds terribly interesting," said Josephine. "How very . . . progressive for a school to teach girls about . . . transportation."

"Yes," Scarlet agreed, unsure what *progressive* meant or why the flotsam her cousin was trying to help her. She bet Josephine and Cecily would get along splendidly. "It is."

After that, she made a good effort to hold her tongue and concentrate on not spilling anything. And eventually, dinner came to an end. The grown-ups stood up and moved to the sitting room to discuss how lucrative Humphries's plantation was.

"Miss Scarlet," Ben spoke up before she could follow. "I think there's a book in the library you might find interesting. It's about carts," he added. "Big ones, small ones, ones with . . . wheels."

"Oh!" Scarlet stopped. "Good. I do love a good book about carts."

"I'll come, too." Cecily stood up, smoothing out her skirt. Scarlet rolled her eyes.

"But I was hoping you could show me the collection of hair clips you mentioned earlier," Josephine said. "It sounds wonderful."

"Oh." Cecily looked from Josephine to Ben to Scarlet. "Well, all right. It's upstairs. We'll just be a few minutes," she added to Ben.

"Take your time," he told her, and she tossed Scarlet a tiny glare.

Safe inside the library, Ben shut the door, then turned to face her, hands on hips. "All right, McCray, what the flotsam are you doing?"

She opened her mouth to answer, but he went on.

"Why aren't you with the crew? And when did you leave them for your father?"

"I didn't leave them for my father," she snapped. "How could you think that? I'd never leave the crew. Not like some people," she added, for she'd had quite enough of being bullied by . . . by landlubbers!

Ben flinched, then gritted his teeth. "And yet, here you are." He spread his arms wide.

"Not because I want to be," she retorted. "This is only for a few weeks. Trust me, I'd never set foot on a plantation if I had a choice." She glared daggers at him.

Ben tossed them right back. "There's a new pirate captain out there, you know. He's planning to take over the entire tropics. They call him—"

"The Rebel," Scarlet finished. "And I call him Lucas Lawrence."

Ben's mouth fell open, and Scarlet rejoiced at having one-upped him. "Lucas?"

"None other," she replied. "And don't worry, we're taking care of it." That last part wasn't true, of course, but she couldn't have him thinking she needed his advice.

Ben sat down in an armchair, looking dizzy. "I heard . . . I heard he was getting a new ship. And calling it the *Panther*."

She shrugged, not particularly caring what Lucas decided to call his ship. She still wasn't done with Ben. "You don't need to tell me anything, Hodgins," she said. "I'm still living my mission. I haven't abandoned ship."

He looked as if she'd hit him, and for a moment she almost felt bad. Then she remembered one more thing.

"And while we're on the topic, why don't you come clean? Does your plantation keep slaves or not?"

Deep down, she hadn't really believed it possible. Ben, her former captain, managing slaves?

So when his face clouded over again, and he stared at the floor, her mouth fell wide open.

"You've *got* to be kidding me."

Just then the door opened, and in walked Humphries, followed by Uncle Daniel and Admiral McCray.

"Ben! Scarlet!" Humphries looked surprised. "What are you doing in here?"

There was a long pause, then Ben said, "Looking for a book." He turned around to browse the books on the shelf before taking one down and handing it to Scarlet. "About carts. To help Scarlet's . . . schooling."

Scarlet looked at the cover. *A Young Lady's Guide to Embroidery*. Not even close. But she couldn't say anything. She was still reeling at what she'd just learned.

Humphries gave them an odd look, then shrugged and walked over to his desk. "Daniel and John and I were just having a fascinating conversation. Did you know, Ben, that John was married to an Islander at one point? An Islander! Can you believe it?"

Scarlet relieved Ben of her dagger glare and turned it on Humphries instead.

Ben looked from Humphries to John, then back at Scarlet, and she suddenly realized that she'd never told him about her past. Back then, she'd barely remembered it herself.

"I see." Ben frowned. "I'm sorry for your loss, Admiral McCray."

Her father acknowledged him with a nod. He looked tired, Scarlet noted. Talking to Humphries for hours probably had that effect on everyone.

Humphries pulled a pipe out of a desk drawer and lit it. "It just astounds me, John, that you would have left port to live in the wilds of some island with those people. Did you actually go barefoot? And wear leaves for clothing?" He laughed. "What a fascinating life you must have led."

The back of Scarlet's neck began to tingle, as if somewhere out there, Voodoo Miranda was sticking pins into a wax doll with her name on it. The admiral pressed his lips together and didn't answer.

"They were indeed fascinating people," echoed Uncle Daniel. "And such a tragic story. The Islanders knew everything about plant cures, didn't they? To think, all that knowledge died with them."

"The Islanders' demise was tragic for more reasons than that," Scarlet pointed out, and her father's eyes flicked over to her. But he didn't even bother reprimanding her.

And anyway, Humphries didn't seem to hear. He pointed his pipe at Uncle Daniel. "I never thought of it like that."

Uncle Daniel nodded. "There are so many undiscovered medicines in the jungle. There might well be something in there that could cure the plague back home."

Something that could have cured his wife, Scarlet thought. Then another thought occurred to her: *And maybe keep his daughter safe, too.* Maybe *that* was why Uncle Daniel was so afraid for Josephine's health.

Humphries puffed on his pipe. "Interesting," he said slowly. "Can you imagine how much money one could make off a cure like that? I bet it would be a lucrative business."

Scarlet gagged, then tried to cover it with a cough.

"Scarlet?" Uncle Daniel turned to her. "Are you all right?"

"No," she replied between gritted teeth. "No, I'm not feeling so well. I bet it was the soup."

"Would you like to go home now, Scarlet?" asked her father, who obviously wanted to be there himself.

She nodded. "Please."

"Well, that's unfortunate," said Humphries. "We'll have to continue this conversation another time. I'll have the butler fetch the girls."

Scarlet avoided Ben's eyes as they filed back out to the carriage and drove away. Her brain still reeled at her latest discovery—that her former captain now worked for someone who kept slaves.

Don't think about it, she told herself. *It doesn't matter.* She had bigger things to think about than a family of Old Worlders who thought themselves better than everyone else. If she never saw any of them again, it would be too soon.

CHAPTER TEN

"How's this?" Liam clapped both halves of a coconut shell together.

"Good," said Jem. He shook the gourd he'd hollowed out and filled with seeds. "Kapu?"

Seated on the jungle floor beside them, Kapu held up his own noisemaker—several wooden pipes that hung from a block of wood and made a hollow chiming sound when shaken.

The boys played their noisemakers all at once, as loud as they could.

"All right, already!" Tim yelled from his seat in the tree above their heads. "You're giving me a headache."

Jem set his instrument down and looked up at the quartermaster, who still hadn't recovered from Uncle Finn stealing the *Hop* the day before. "How's the wire coming?" he called.

"Almost done. Keep your trousers on," Tim grumbled. A moment later, he jumped down to the ground. "There."

Jem stood and squinted up at the trap they'd created thanks to Kapu's creative thinking. They'd installed it on the narrowest part of the path, so the panther would have to pass over it on his way to the tree houses. A trip wire on the ground would set off the noisemakers in the tree, effectively scaring the beast away. "Think it'll work?"

Tim shrugged. "You think your uncle will be back today?"

Jem sighed. "I don't know, Swig. If not today, probably tomorrow." Of course, he had no idea when Uncle Finn would be back with the *Hop*. And frankly, the ship's absence hadn't made much difference to anyone except Tim—they had no plans to go to port until Scarlet was ready to come home, and that wouldn't be for another few weeks. But that kind of logic would only make the quartermaster even grouchier. So he left it at that.

"It's just . . ." Tim took off his spectacles and wiped them on his shirt. "I'm worried he's not treating her right. Her wheel needs a special touch, and I'm sure Uncle Finn doesn't have it. See, sometimes she lists to starboard, and—"

"Blimey, Swig," Liam cut in. "Quit worrying. I'm sure Uncle Finn knows how to steer a ship."

"I'm not!" Tim pushed his spectacles back on and glared at Liam. "He's a scientist, not a navigator. And . . . and he just had no right to take her!" He turned his glare on Jem.

Jem took a deep breath and counted to five. "Swig," he said for perhaps the tenth time in two days, "if I'd known he was going to take the *Hop,* I would have stopped him. But I didn't know, any more than you did. And there's nothing we can do now except wait until he gets back."

"*If* he gets back," Tim said darkly. He turned and marched away.

Jem rolled his eyes and turned back to Liam and

Kapu. "All right. Let's add these to the collection up there." He pointed to the cluster of noisemakers already suspended from Tim's wire.

"Kapu!" Smitty came running through the trees, emerging breathless beside them. "Kapu! I heard the news! Is she all right?"

"What news?" Jem and Liam turned from Smitty to Kapu. "What's wrong?"

"It's Sina," Smitty panted. "She's . . . sick."

"Really?" Jem looked at Kapu. This was the first he'd heard of her illness.

Kapu shrugged and pointed at his head. Then he put both hands together and used them as a pillow, pretending to sleep.

"She has a headache?" Liam asked. Kapu nodded.

"That's all?" Jem looked at Smitty, who shook his head.

"It's terrible," he said. "I need to go see her. I'll . . . I'll sing her back to health."

Kapu shook his head violently.

"Don't think that's a good idea, Smit." Liam grinned.

"Why not?" asked Smitty. "I think she needs me."

Kapu shook his head again, then held up a finger, instructing them to watch. First he pretended to be Sina, sleeping peacefully. Then he pretended to be Smitty, warbling off-key. Then he was Sina again, lunging for Smitty's throat and shaking him violently.

Jem laughed. "Sounds like she's a bit grumpy when she's under the weather."

Smitty considered this. "Okay, so I won't sing. I'll just

bring her some nice flowers. She'll like that, right?"

Kapu shook his head again. This time he mimed Sina reaching for her bow and arrow and aiming it at Smitty's head.

"Come on, Smit," said Jem. "Help us put the finishing touches on this trap for the panther. Then we'll test it out."

Smitty looked around at the wires and noisemakers, and he shook his head. "I have a feeling she needs me. I'm going to go check up on her, anyway."

Kapu shrugged as if to say, "Suit yourself," and the older boy turned and walked away. As he disappeared, they could hear the strains of his latest song:

> *My darling is under the weather.*
> *Kapu says that makes her angry,*
> *But I'm sure that when we're together,*
> *She won't feel like strangling me.*

Jem sneaked toward the trip wire, pretending to be a panther on the hunt. Gingerly, he reached a "paw" into the pile of leaves he and Liam had used to cover it. All of a sudden, a clatter erupted above him, as gourds shook and shells clapped and hollowed sticks rattled together.

Jem covered his ears until the noise subsided. Then he looked up at Liam and Kapu, who were both grinning.

"Works like a charm," he said, hopping to his feet. "Nice work!"

They were still congratulating themselves on their handiwork when they reached the clearing, where a few

Lost Souls were dangling their feet in the pool, cooling themselves in the midafternoon heat.

Jem stopped when he spotted Ronagh sitting cross-legged in the grass with a long-haired monkey on her lap. Two other monkeys sat beside her, as if waiting their turn. "Liam, what's your sister doing?" he asked.

Liam squinted at his sister, then replied, "Looks like she's giving the monkeys haircuts."

"Of course she is." Jem shook his head. At least she was being useful. Or rather, at least she was staying out of trouble.

"Hey, look!" Liam pointed at a person walking across the clearing toward them. "It's Sina."

The Islander girl still looked a little tired when she joined them.

"Feeling better?" Jem asked, pointing at his head.

Sina nodded.

"Did Smitty's medicine work?" Liam laughed, and Kapu translated the question for Sina, who looked confused. She shook her head and said something back. Kapu looked startled.

"What?" Jem asked. "What is it?"

Kapu pretended to be Smitty, delivering flowers and singing a song. Then he shook his head and shrugged, looking around.

"What?" said Jem. "What does that mean? Where is he?"

"I think he means Smitty didn't go see Sina," said Liam, and Kapu nodded. "That's funny. He was so set on seeing her."

"That *is* funny," Jem agreed. In fact, it was downright strange.

"Maybe we should go look for him," said Liam.

"Look for who?" Ronagh asked, joining them. A monkey sat on her shoulder, patting its new spiky hairstyle.

"Smitty," said Liam. "He was on his way to visit Sina but never made it."

"Maybe he got lost?" Ronagh suggested.

"It's a pretty straight path," Jem said. "And Smitty knows it well." His stomach began to feel heavy. As far as he knew, only two things could keep Smitty from Sina. One was a pirate. The other was a panther. "Let's go," he said.

Sina, Kapu, Liam, and Ronagh followed him to the edge of the jungle, then down the path back to the Islanders' house.

"Smitty!" Jem and Ronagh called into the trees.

"Milton!" Liam added. "Evander!"

Jem frowned at him. "Is now really the time?"

Liam shrugged. "You never know when you're going to get it right."

They moved farther into the jungle, scanning the trail and the trees for clues. Sina fitted an arrow to her bow and moved out in front, ready to shoot if necessary. By now, Jem's stomach felt like someone had filled it with rocks. He couldn't help but wonder which would be worse—the pirate or the panther. On the one hand, they knew how to fight off pirates. On the other hand, they'd never had to deal with a pirate who wanted to enslave them. Suppose that was what had happened to Smitty? Suppose Lucas was holding him captive, forcing him to swab the deck with a toothbrush? Or maybe he'd make him into a powder monkey, the one forced to carry power to the guns. It was the most dangerous job on board a ship, and one—

"Look!" Ronagh cried suddenly, pointing off the side of the trail. The group stopped and huddled around the spot she was indicating. The rocks in Jem's stomach turned a flip.

There, in the dirt, not three hundred yards from camp, was the biggest, deepest panther print he'd ever seen.

Sina gasped and pointed to a brambly bush just off the path. Hooked to a prickle was a piece of gray fabric. A piece of—

"Smitty's trousers," Ronagh breathed.

"No!" Jem exclaimed, kneeling to inspect the fabric. But Ronagh was right. He'd seen the boy wearing those very trousers, not two hours before. "And look!" Next to the brambly bush lay an abandoned bouquet of slightly wilted flowers.

He began to wish that it had been a pirate.

"Shivers," Ronagh whispered. "Smitty's been . . . catnapped!"

CHAPTER ELEVEN

Scarlet waited until the merchant was busy haggling with a customer, then reached out and grabbed a compass off his table of wares. She slipped it into her trouser pocket and strolled on.

To be out of her dress and back into her cabin boy clothes felt nothing short of delicious. She could walk without limping, run without petticoats bunching up, steal things without . . . well, she couldn't possibly have stolen *anything* while wearing a dress. Where would she have hidden her plunder? She shoved her hands in her pockets and whistled one of Smitty's chanteys.

Any guilt she'd felt about lying to her father that morning had long since disappeared. He might have seen through her anyway, when she'd refused to get out of bed, claiming that she had a splitting headache.

Josephine had helped, too, although unknowingly. She'd stood by Scarlet's bed that morning, pressing her hand against Scarlet's forehead. "She can't go with us today, Uncle John," she'd concluded. "She looks terrible."

Scarlet nodded, although she hadn't thought she looked *that* bad. "You go on and visit that Right Honorable What's-his-name without me. And his Right Honorable rose gardens." She coughed for effect.

The admiral narrowed his eyes at her, but he didn't

argue. He might still have been feeling bad about the conversation with Humphries the night before.

Josephine ushered him out, closing the door softly behind them and leaving Scarlet triumphantly punching the air in the darkness. She waited until they'd breakfasted and left to visit that Right Honorable Whoever-he-was, then hopped out of bed, flung open the door, and danced a jig right there in her nightgown.

"A morning to myself!" she sang. "No embroidery, no visiting, no cutlery! And NO DRESSES!"

The last few hours had been jolly indeed. No one chastised her for tromping through mud puddles. No one frowned when she snagged her sleeve on a wire fence and ripped a hole right through it. In fact, no one looked at her at all now that she looked like every other sailor in port. And that suited her just fine. She had work to do.

"I heard he recruited the Blood Brothers, Blair and Blake," a cabin boy told her when she asked him about Lucas.

"Hmm." Scarlet pursed her lips. The Blood Brothers were best known—and feared—for their back-to-back sword-fighting skills. "Anything else?"

The boy shook his head. "Maybe some of them know." He jerked his thumb in the direction of the docks, where half a dozen pirates were gathered, deep in conversation.

Scarlet let the boy go with a nod of thanks. She sauntered toward the pirates and stationed herself within eavesdropping distance.

"Ye don't say!" one of them exclaimed.

"That wee plant can do all that?"

"If ingested correctly, yes," said a familiar voice. "Now, I highly recommend you take it with food, and always at the same time of day. Check back with me in three days time, and I'll—"

"Uncle Finn!" Scarlet exclaimed. She'd know his posh Old World accent anywhere.

She waited impatiently while the pirates snatched up their plant samples and dispersed, leaving Uncle Finn and Thomas standing on the docks, looking pleased. It took every drop of Scarlet's willpower not to run over and hug them. Instead, she sauntered over, hands in her pockets, trying not to grin too widely.

"Scarlet!" Thomas exclaimed when he saw her. "Er . . . I mean, cabin boy I've never seen before." He gave her an exaggerated wink.

Uncle Finn shook his head at his assistant, then greeted Scarlet with a warm handshake. "How are you, dear?" he whispered.

"Surviving," she replied. "How's the crew? Has there been any trouble with Lucas? Or the panther?"

"No sign of either," Uncle Finn reported, and she relaxed. "We're just here for a few days, testing our samples on some pirates."

"That's good," she said. "But how did you get here? Did Tim bring you?" She couldn't believe her quartermaster hadn't stopped by to say hello.

"No," Uncle Finn said. "We came by ourselves."

"In the *Hop*?" she asked, and they nodded. "Tim let you take the *Hop* without him?"

"Not exactly . . ." Thomas began.

"The crew agreed that we should go to port," Uncle Finn said.

"You took it without telling them?" Scarlet cried.

"No," Uncle Finn huffed. "They all insisted we go to port. I was surprised, too, but I wasn't about to argue."

Scarlet raised an eyebrow. She highly doubted that her crew would have let the explorers take the *Hop*, leaving them shipless on Island X. But before she could ask any more questions, something even more odd caught her attention.

It was an old man hobbling by, bent over a cane. At least, she thought it was an old man, but she couldn't say for sure, since he was dressed head to toe in a black cloak, not unlike the ones the Lost Souls used to wear on ship raids. She'd never seen anyone like this in port before.

"Excuse me, will you?" she said, and the explorers waved her off, turning once again to their plant samples.

She followed the old man off the docks and across the road, falling in line a safe distance behind him. There was something very strange about him. She studied him closely until it came to her—he kept changing the way he limped, almost as if he kept forgetting which foot he'd hurt.

If he's a lame old man, then I'm a proper lady, thought Scarlet.

It came as no surprise that his destination was none other than Voodoo Miranda's house. Scarlet followed him right up to the front porch, then hid behind an abandoned barrel while he rapped at the door.

The door squeaked open, and Miranda peered out, this time with a boa constrictor draped around her neck.

Seeing the voodoo queen, the man took a quick step back, dropping his cane.

"Wait a minute . . . ," Scarlet murmured. Would a *friend* of Miranda's be so surprised by her pet snake?

Voodoo Miranda gave her visitor a once-over, then stroked the snake's head. "Captain Wallace," she said, sounding a bit bored. "Why the costume?"

Scarlet gasped. The Dread Pirate Captain Wallace Hammerstein-Jones! She stretched her neck to get a better view.

Captain Wallace straightened and raised a finger to his lips. "Shh," he said. "I need your help."

"Obviously," said Miranda. Then she sighed. "All right, come in. But mind the boa. He hasn't eaten in a week, and he's a little peckish."

Captain Wallace gulped and darted past the snake. Miranda closed the door behind him.

"Blimey!" Scarlet cried, standing up. "What's that all about?" Then she remembered the little window in Miranda's kitchen. If she could find it, maybe she could figure out what the flotsam was going on.

She zipped around the side of the house and pressed herself flat up against the wall. The first window she shuffled past looked into a room she hadn't seen before—one filled with animals that had once been alive but were now stuffed and frozen in strange positions. A smelly wild pig stared down an iguana. An enormous brown monkey raised its arms as if trying to scare off a predator.

Scarlet shuddered and moved on.

The next window looked into a room that was nearly empty except for a table, a chair, and a tall candlestick. And . . . Scarlet squinted hard . . . a wax figurine lying flat on the table, pins sticking out of its stomach. She shuddered again. That must have hurt.

Finally, she found the cloudy little window that looked into the kitchen. And as luck would have it, it was open. Just a crack, but enough for her to catch their conversation.

"Biscuit?" Miranda offered Captain Wallace a plate of gray lumps that looked vaguely like the cookies she'd offered Scarlet days before.

The captain took off his hood, revealing a still-sunburned face and a greasy mop of hair. "Don't mind if I do." He reached for one and popped it in his mouth. "So."

"So." Miranda unwound the boa from her neck and set it down on the counter.

Captain Wallace scraped his chair a few inches away. "I need your help," he said.

"So you said. Revenge?"

The captain nodded. "How did you know?"

Miranda waved her hand. "Everyone wants revenge. Also, you look a little desperate."

"Oh, I am," said the captain. "You have no idea."

"Mm-hm." Miranda broke a biscuit in half and nibbled at it. "Let me guess. Lucas Lawrence."

Captain Wallace nodded. "That . . . that . . . biscuit-eater."

Miranda stopped nibbling her biscuit and raised an eyebrow at him.

"Oh. Sorry. I didn't mean . . . These are actually very good biscuits. What kind did you say they were?"

"I didn't," said Miranda. "They're beetle biscuits."

The captain turned pale. "Beetle?" He peered down at the black flecks in the biscuits, which from Scarlet's vantage point looked like raisins. Her stomach pitched.

"Right, well, what do you have in mind?" asked the voodoo queen. "Stomachache? Kidney stones? Bunions? Bunions are always good."

The captain shook his head. "I want more. That boy shamed me in front of everyone. I want to make him pay."

Scarlet shivered.

Miranda looked at Captain Wallace for a moment, then tapped her purple lips with a finger. "Tell you what I'll do. I'll give you something better than voodoo."

"Oh?" Captain Wallace leaned forward on his elbows.

Miranda nodded. "I'll give you information."

"Oh." The captain leaned back, disappointed. "Really? Because maybe bunions would be more effective."

"Quiet," said Miranda. "Listen. Your enemy has a plan. He aims to call his new ship—"

"The *Panther*," Captain Wallace finished. "I *know*."

She glared at him. "You want my information or not?"

He paused, then nodded.

"Then shut it," said Miranda. "What you don't know is that Captain Lucas aims to get a pet."

"A pet?" Scarlet repeated, then ducked after realizing she'd spoken aloud. A *pet*? Back on the *Hop*, there had been a "no pets" rule, and Lucas had never seemed too bothered by it. She rose back up slowly and peered through the window again.

Captain Wallace looked bewildered. "Why should I care about Lucas getting a pet?" he spat.

"Because you don't know what kind of pet it is." Miranda helped herself to another biscuit.

Captain Wallace raised an eyebrow. "What is it?"

Miranda took her time chewing and swallowing, then picked a beetle out of her teeth. "What does Captain Lucas plan to name his new ship?" she asked.

"The *Pan*—" Captain Wallace stopped. "Oh."

"Sink me," said Scarlet. "A—"

"Panther," said Voodoo Miranda. "The boy thinks it'll be the perfect companion for the fiercest pirate in the tropics. He hasn't gotten it yet, but my sources tell me he's heading off tomorrow to capture it."

"B-b-but," Captain Wallace sputtered. "Where will he get a p-panther?"

Miranda brushed off her crumbs and stood up. "I believe you once had a map that told you that."

Captain Wallace's eyes lit up. "A map of—"

"Island X," Scarlet finished. "Oh *no*," she added.

"Oh yes." Captain Wallace stood and started to pace. "A panther's lair. Yes, I remember now. I bet I could find it, even without the map he stole. And maybe . . ." He paused, tapping his chin. "Maybe I could *sabotage* his plans. Maybe I could *trap* him in the lair. But I'm going to need a crew of my own, of course. A fierce one, like Lucas's—"

Scarlet had heard all she needed to. She had to get home. Not to her father's home, but to Island X. Where her two greatest enemies were headed, and her crew was completely oblivious.

CHAPTER TWELVE

Scarlet was so deep in thought as she walked back to her father's house that she didn't notice the carriage until it was just a few yards away. She stopped and blinked hard. It was her father's carriage, parked right outside his front door.

Which meant that he, Uncle Daniel, and Josephine were already home.

"Blast!" Scarlet cried. She ought to be in bed or at least draped dramatically across the parlor sofa.

She did an about-turn and zipped back around the corner, over a fence, and into the alley behind the house. She barged through the back door and into the kitchen, elbowing a maid out of the way and jostling the cook, who dropped an entire bag of salt into the soup she was making. Ignoring their shrieks, she ran on, taking the back stairs three at a time. Only at the top of the stairs did she stop to catch her breath.

Slowly, she opened the door to the upstairs hallway. It was empty, but she could hear voices in the library.

"Those gardens were spectacular," Uncle Daniel was saying. "The gardener must have reams of plant knowledge."

"But probably not the kind of knowledge you're looking for," said the admiral. "I doubt he knows about plant cures."

That was it, then. Uncle Daniel was looking for a cure for the plague. Likely that was why the king had sent him here in the first place. It made Scarlet uneasy to think about Old Worlders combing the jungles for medicines. But now wasn't the time to ponder it.

She took off her boots and tiptoed across the hallway, then slipped into her bedroom.

"Whew," she breathed, closing the door behind her. "Safe. That was a—" She stopped as her eyes fell upon Josephine's coat, spread out on the foot of her perfectly made bed. It hadn't been there when Scarlet had left that morning, she was sure of it. Which could only mean that Josephine had come straight to their bedroom when she got home. Which could only mean that she'd seen Scarlet's bed empty.

"Blimey!" Scarlet smacked her forehead. Her father was going to slay her. She was fish food.

She took a deep breath. *Not that it matters now,* she told herself. *All that matters is that I leave tonight. Father can be as angry as he wants—it won't change anything.*

She changed out of her shirt and trousers and into the simplest dress in the closet, then headed for the library. She didn't need a mirror to tell her she looked like she'd been swept up by a hurricane, but neither did she care. She just had to make it through the day so she could leave that night when everyone was asleep. *Don't think,* she reminded herself. *Just do.*

"Scarlet," her father said when she appeared at the door. "How are you?" He didn't look angry, or even suspicious. She faltered a bit, then stepped inside.

"Um, I'm . . . feeling better," she said slowly. It was impossible to tell how much he knew or suspected.

"You missed a very pleasant visit, dear," said Uncle Daniel. "The gardens were stupendous. I'm continually impressed by how people can cultivate so many plants in this climate. I keep saying it, but the tropics are just so full of potential."

Out of the corner of her eye, Scarlet thought she saw her father give his brother a hard look.

"How is your headache?" Josephine asked. Her face was easy to read. Her lips were pressed tightly together, and her eyes practically bored holes right into Scarlet's.

"Oh." Scarlet looked away. "It's . . . better." She cringed at the lie and tried to send Josephine a silent apology, the way she communicated with Sina.

Josephine walked away to look out the window.

It doesn't matter, Scarlet told herself throughout the afternoon, while Josephine sat by the window, knitting what appeared to be a small gray mouse and avoiding Scarlet's eye. *What matters is the island, not your Old World cousin.*

Whatever Josephine was feeling would not stand in the way of Scarlet getting home before Lucas and Captain Wallace arrived.

"Scarlet." Her father stopped her on her way to bed, pulling her into the library and shutting the door behind him.

"Yes?" She swallowed hard, steeling herself for a

lecture, or worse. She tried to focus on her escape plan, which she would put into action as soon as everyone fell asleep.

"I just wanted to say . . ." He paused, then put both hands on her shoulders. "I'm proud of you."

"What?" Scarlet took a step back. "Why?"

"These past few days haven't been easy, but your effort has been admirable. Daniel and Josephine adore you. They don't suspect a thing."

"Well, I don't know about that." She looked down at her boots.

"They've had a difficult time, those two," said the admiral. "Josephine's mother's death took quite a toll on them, as you and I can appreciate."

"Right," Scarlet said, now feeling even guiltier for lying to her cousin. But what could she have done differently?

It doesn't matter, she reminded herself. *All that matters tonight is the island.* But even she didn't quite believe it anymore.

"You look tired," her father said. "Go to bed now, and sleep well, my dear."

She obeyed, trying not to think about how she was about to let him down, too. Being part of a family was just too hard.

Scarlet waited until Josephine's breathing grew deep and even in the bed beside hers. Then she waited a few minutes more before peeling off her covers and swinging her legs out of bed. The moon shone through the tiny window between their beds, illuminating her path to the closet, where her cabin boy clothes were stashed. She changed quickly, tucking her dagger inside her old boots.

Uncle Finn should never have taken the *Hop* without asking, but she was awfully glad he had. Now she had a way home, and although she'd never captained it by herself before, she was fairly certain she could—

"Where are you going?"

Scarlet yelped and spun around. Josephine was sitting up in bed, eyes wide and shining in the moonlight.

"Oh. Um."

"And *why* are you dressed like a boy?" Josephine folded her hands in her lap and regarded Scarlet dead-on.

"Well." Scarlet swallowed hard. "I'm just headed out for a midnight stroll. I do that sometimes. I'm an . . . in . . . insom . . . I don't sleep well."

Josephine kept staring at her. "I see. Is that what you were doing today while we were out?"

"Oh. Um. Yes?" Scarlet grimaced. Josephine had every right to demand an explanation, but Scarlet couldn't very well explain it all *now*. "Look, Josephine, I have to go. Can we discuss this—"

Josephine reached over and lit the lamp on the table between their beds. "Tell me the truth," she said. "Now."

Scarlet started. "The truth? But . . . but I did. I'm an in . . . an im . . ."

Josephine hopped out of bed and looked Scarlet square in the eye. "The truth," she said. "No more lies, Scarlet. I think we can both agree that this has gone on long enough."

For a moment, Scarlet had half a mind to burst out the window and rappel down to the ground, as if escaping a ship she'd been raiding. But the window was too small, and she didn't have any ropes, and anyway, Josephine's stare was holding her in place.

"All right." She sighed. "But let's make this quick."

Josephine folded her arms across her chest.

"I'm not who I said I am," Scarlet began. "I'm not a lady or . . . or anything like it. In fact, I spend most of my time dressed like a boy, like this. I . . . I'm a pirate."

Josephine did a double take. She obviously hadn't expected *that*. "A . . . a . . ."

"Pirate," Scarlet repeated. "At least, I used to be. Now I'm, well, I'm the guardian of one of these islands—the island where I was born. Remember the jungle I described to you the other day?"

Josephine nodded.

"That's where I live, and there's nothing in the world I love more than it. Tomorrow morning it's going to be invaded. So I'm going back, right now, to protect it."

Josephine looked at Scarlet as if she wasn't sure whether to believe her or scream for their fathers. Without taking her eyes off her, she sank back down on the bed.

"I know this doesn't make sense to you, and I'd explain better if I had more time," Scarlet said. "Tell you what. If I can, I'll come back before you leave, and I'll explain everything then. Of course, it might be better if I stayed away, since my father's going to kill me for running away, but . . ." She trailed off, distracted by the image of her father's frown. Then she snapped back to the present. "I'm sorry I lied to you. It's actually been . . . nice . . . getting to know you. Even though, you know, we're so different."

Josephine didn't reply. They stared at each other for a moment, then Scarlet shrugged and turned to leave. She opened the door slowly.

"You don't think I'm just going to let you leave, do you?"

Scarlet whirled around. Josephine was standing with her hands on her hips. Scarlet closed the door.

"Sorry, what?"

"I'm not letting you leave."

Despite the urgency of the situation, Scarlet almost laughed. "*You're* going to stop *me*?"

Josephine drew herself up and stuck out her chin. "Not exactly," she said. "I'm going with you."

CHAPTER THIRTEEN

"You can't be serious."

Josephine was unsettlingly calm. "I *am* serious. I'm going with you."

Scarlet almost grabbed her cousin by the shoulders and shook her. "Look. Josephine. You don't understand. My home is very . . . uncomfortable. There are no beds. There is no cutlery. And there are lots of bugs. Big, *nasty* bugs."

Josephine considered this, then nodded. "I'll be all right."

Scarlet closed her eyes and counted to five. "Let me try this again. You won't like the journey. We have to sail for several hours on choppy seas, then hike through a jungle for several more. It'll be hot. And it'll be dirty. And it'll be *dangerous*." She tried to keep her voice down, although she really wanted to scream.

Josephine swallowed hard but smiled again. "I'll be fine. Don't worry about me."

Scarlet groaned and pulled off her cap, twisting it in her hands. "But . . . but *why*? Why would you want to come?"

"Well . . ." Josephine thought for a moment. "I suppose because I want to see who you really are."

"Then let me *tell* you!" Scarlet cried. "But not now. I'll explain everything later."

Josephine shook her head. "I'm coming. And . . . and if you don't let me, I can easily wake my father right now. And yours, too."

Scarlet's mouth fell open. "You wouldn't."

Josephine pressed her lips together.

"Okay, fine!" Scarlet threw her hands in the air. "You can come. But you can't slow me down, or . . . or I'll leave you behind."

"I won't." Josephine darted to the closet. "Just let me get dressed."

While her cousin pulled on a pink dress more suited to a Sunday picnic than a pirate ship, Scarlet paced the room. "I can't believe I'm doing this," she muttered to herself. "Father's going to kill me. Uncle Daniel's going to kill me. The crew is going to kill me." She could only imagine what the Lost Souls would think of her prim and proper cousin. She opened her mouth to protest again, but Josephine cut her off.

"I'm coming," she said simply.

Scarlet shook her head. If Uncle Daniel had wanted Josephine to broaden her horizons in the tropics, he definitely hadn't had this in mind.

"All right," Josephine said a few minutes later. "I'm ready." Her hair was neatly braided and her boots were tightly laced. Boy clothes would have been better, but there was no time for that.

They tiptoed out the door and down the hall, stopping at the library so Scarlet could scribble a note to her father.

Danger at home, she wrote. *Had to go. If not back in a few days, come find me.*

She paused, remembering their conversation earlier that night. He'd be disappointed in her. Possibly very angry, too. But *maybe* he'd understand? She added, *P.S. I'm sorry.*

Then she remembered the most important part.

P.P.S. Josephine came, too. I'm really sorry.

She slipped the note under his bedroom door and tiptoed down the stairs and out the front door, Josephine close behind.

The air was warm and filled with firefly flickers and the buzz of cicadas from the jungle nearby. Scarlet turned to Josephine. "One more chance to turn back."

Josephine shook her head. "I'm coming."

"Fine," said Scarlet. "Can you run in that?" She pointed to Josephine's skirt.

"Yes." Josephine hiked it up, and they took off for the docks.

"Th-this is . . . yours?" Josphine whispered.

Scarlet stopped rowing and balanced the oars across the dinghy they'd "borrowed." "Not mine, exactly. It belongs to the Lost Souls," she said, watching the *Hop* bob slowly in the inky water. She reached out and gave it a quick pat.

Thank you, she told it silently, then looked up at the stars overhead. *And thank you, Uncle Finn, for taking the ship without asking.* He'd be baffled when he found it missing the next day, but that was the least of her worries. "Come on," she said to Josephine.

"But . . . but how?" Josephine asked, squinting up at the ship. "Do we have to climb?" Her voice trembled a bit.

"Yes," said Scarlet. "But it's not that hard. Watch." She pulled out the grappling iron she'd also borrowed, then launched it into the air. It hooked onto the side rail, and Scarlet had to grin. After nearly a week of floundering at everything ladylike, she was back in her element.

She demonstrated how to climb aboard using the rope attached to the iron, then climbed down and watched as Josephine attempted it, shaking with every step.

Halfway up, her cousin paused. "Are you sure about this?" she called down, voice trembling.

"Don't look down," Scarlet commanded. "You're doing well. Just a few more steps."

"'Just a few more steps,'" Josephine repeated to herself, and she started climbing again.

Scarlet had to hand it to her cousin—she had determination. If only Uncle Daniel could see her.

Once Josephine was safely on board, Scarlet scampered up after her.

Setting sail took five times longer than usual, since there was only one of her to raise the sails and weigh anchor. Josephine offered to help, but it took as long to explain what she needed to do as it did to do it herself. And there was no time to lose.

Once they were safely out of port, Scarlet stopped to catch her breath. She leaned against the wheel and closed her eyes for just a moment.

"I have a question," Josephine said suddenly.

Scarlet shook herself awake and nodded. "All right."

"Does your father know . . . about all this?" Josephine spread her arms wide.

"He does." Scarlet considered telling her everything, even about her father's mission to protect the island, but then she remembered Uncle Daniel's devotion to the king. "The island is his home, too," she said simply.

"And what about that boy at the plantation. Ben?" Josephine's eyes narrowed. "You two . . . seemed to know each other."

Scarlet nodded. "He was captain when I came aboard."

"But . . . but he looked so . . . dignified," Josephine said, mystified.

Scarlet snorted. "You should have seen him a few years back. His hair used to get so matted that we'd have to shave it all off. And once, an entire family of bugs started nesting in his ear."

"No!" Josephine shrieked. "That's disgusting!" She shuddered, then admitted, "I thought he might have been your boyfriend."

"Boyfriend!" Scarlet exploded. "Not bloody likely!"

Josephine flinched.

"Sorry," Scarlet said. "Ben was my captain and nothing more. I admired him, of course, but . . ." She felt her ears grow hot and looked away, out to sea. "Anyway, now he's nothing."

Josephine stayed quiet for a while, taking everything in. Eventually she said, "You know, I always knew there was more to you than met the eye, but I certainly didn't expect *this*."

Scarlet had to smile at that. "I guess I've thrown a lot at you today," she said.

"Yes," Josephine agreed.

They fell silent again as Scarlet navigated the ship through the black waves, and Josephine studied her every move.

"You're not seasick?" Scarlet asked.

Josephine shook her head. "I don't get seasick."

"But what about on the trip from the Old World? When you arrived, Uncle Daniel said you'd been sick."

Josephine sighed. "I was fine. My father just worries."

Scarlet turned the wheel gently. "Because of your mother?"

Josephine nodded. "He means well. He's just afraid I'll get sick like she did. That's why he brought me with him, actually. Back home, the plague is spreading so quickly."

Scarlet shuddered. She knew that story well. "So that's why he's looking for a cure."

Josephine nodded. "He thinks there must be some undiscovered plant in the jungle. Which might be true, but I'm not sure how he's going to find it."

Scarlet pictured a jungle overrun by Old Worlders searching for plant medicines, and shivered. Of course it was important for them to find a cure for this plague. But did they have to do it in the jungle? Hadn't they done enough damage to the islands already?

"Did your father do the same after your mother died?" Josephine asked, pulling her back to the present.

"No," she replied. "He left me with a governess and

141

went back to the King's Men." She was surprised to find that it still hurt when she said it out loud. Even now, after they'd been reunited and were supposed to be a family again.

"I suppose everyone deals with it in their own way," Josephine said softly.

They sailed on in silence for a few more minutes, both girls staring into the darkness ahead. Eventually, they both agreed in unison, "They're going to kill us."

By the time they dropped anchor off the coast of Island X and began rowing to shore, the sky was just beginning to lighten around the edges. If they hurried, it would be midmorning when they reached the camp to alert the Lost Souls. Scarlet's stomach growled, but she shushed it, for they had nothing to eat.

She looked across the rowboat at her cousin. "You must be starving," she said.

Josephine shrugged and gave her a small smile. "I'll be fine."

"I'll try to find us some fruit on the way," Scarlet promised, then pulled off her boots and slipped into the shallows. She pushed the dinghy to shore, where Josephine could disembark without getting wet.

Josephine gave her a grateful look as she climbed out. "Thank you."

Scarlet tucked her boots under her arm. "It's that way." She pointed into the jungle just beyond the beach. "We've got some climbing ahead of us, but my crew hikes this way all the time, so there's a decent path."

"I still can't get used to the fact that you have a *crew*," Josephine marveled, staring up at the towering trees and tangled vines. Some monkeys swung, screeching, from a branch hanging out over the beach.

"I wouldn't be much of a pirate without a crew," said Scarlet. "You'll meet them soon. And you'll—" She stopped herself before she promised that Josephine would like them. Josephine was hardier than she looked, but the Lost Souls were loud and dirty and full of curse words. Who knew how she'd react to them? "Well, anyway, we should get going."

Josephine looked down at her feet. "You're not going to wear your boots?"

Scarlet made a face. "I despise boots. Barefoot is the only way to go. Look." She lifted up her foot so Josephine could see the sole. "See how tough it is? I barely feel anything underfoot."

Josephine nodded but didn't look convinced.

"Come on." Scarlet turned and led her cousin into the jungle. She rolled her sleeves up past her elbows and took off her cap. It felt good to be home. Well, almost home. She picked up the pace.

They wove their way through the jungle, past the giant tree trunks Scarlet now knew like old friends. Josephine kept up surprisingly well. Her pink dress was streaked with dirt, but she didn't bother to try to clean it. She was breathing heavily but didn't complain about the pace. When a monkey swooped down and pulled one of her curls, she shrieked.

"You!" Scarlet shook her finger at the troublemaker, who swung back up onto a branch above their heads, screaming with laughter. "I remember you. You're the one who got attacked by parrots last month for trying to steal their eggs."

The monkey chattered and waved her arms.

"Well, I'm glad to see that hasn't slowed you down," Scarlet said. "But what the flotsam happened to your hair? It looks like someone . . . cut it?"

The monkey tossed her hair, then screeched and bounded off into the jungle.

"Sorry." Scarlet turned to Josephine, whose mouth had fallen open. "Monkeys can be little terrors sometimes."

"And you *talk* to them?" Josephine asked, bewildered.

"Sometimes," said Scarlet. "But they rarely listen. Come on, let's keep going."

About halfway up the mountain, she spotted two big orange star fruit hanging from a branch several feet above her head. Her stomach grumbled again, and she agreed with it. It would be jolly if she and Josephine could have a star fruit each. But the branch was too high to reach and too thin to hold her if she climbed the tree. She began to search for pebbles to lob at the fruit.

Josephine watched her for a moment, then turned and stepped off the path into the underbrush. She returned moments later with some thin pieces of vine. Without a word, she settled down on the path and started weaving them together.

Scarlet paused with a rock in hand. "Look, um, Josephine," she began, "we're in a bit of a hurry here.

This probably isn't the best time for arts and crafts."

Josephine nodded. "It'll only take a few minutes."

Scarlet bit her tongue to stop herself from arguing. Josephine did deserve a bit of a rest after all Scarlet had put her through. But still, weaving vines in the middle of a journey was pretty . . .

"There!" Josephine held up her creation.

Scarlet looked, blinked, and looked again. It was a small basket, just the right size for star fruit.

"Now all we have to do is find a long stick . . . like this one." Josephine grabbed one lying on the ground nearby. "Then we can hook the basket onto the end. And look!"

Scarlet took the stick and lifted it up so that the basket was directly under the star fruit. Then she gave the fruit a little nudge, and it fell neatly into the basket.

She made a mental note to stop judging Old World education so harshly.

"Well, Josephine," she said as they walked on, nibbling on their breakfast, "that was impressive. I doubt even an Islander could have done better."

Josephine blushed and shook her head. "Oh, that's not true," she said. Then she paused. "But Scarlet . . ."

"Hmm." Scarlet licked a stream of juice off her forearm.

"Maybe . . . maybe now that we're here, you could call me Jo," Josephine suggested. "I've always liked that better."

"Jo." Scarlet smiled. "I like it better, too."

CHAPTER FOURTEEN

When morning finally came, Jem couldn't tell if he'd slept at all. For a moment he shut his eyes and tried to imagine where Scarlet was at that moment. In all likelihood, she was in a warm bed, with breakfast waiting nearby. A real breakfast of toast or porridge and tea, not a handful of nuts and some guava fruit.

What would she do that day? Peruse her father's library? Engage in civilized conversation about current events? Jem pictured his captain in action and concluded that it was unlikely. But whatever she got up to, it probably wouldn't involve trekking across some wild island in search of the man-eating panther that had captured her crewmate.

Groaning, Jem forced himself out of his hammock and sat cross-legged on the floor, head in his hands. Today, he was going to have to face the panther. There was no way around it. He, Jem Fitzgerald, would have to confront a giant predator and ask for his friend back.

In the hammock beside his, Tim muttered something in his sleep, and Jem reached his foot over to kick him awake.

"Too early," Tim moaned.

"Get up," Jem told him. "We've got to make a decision."

"About what?" Tim sat up and rubbed his eyes. "Oh.

Right." He leaned over and shook Liam awake.

"Come on." Jem stood up. "We've got to make a decision. Now."

The Lost Souls had spent the entire previous day scouring the jungle for signs of Smitty. But other than a few more giant paw prints, they hadn't found a trace. Which meant one of two things: Either the panther had gobbled Smitty up on the spot, or he'd taken the boy back to his lair. Jem was choosing to believe that Smitty was still alive and simply keeping the panther company. Which didn't make much sense, but he was trying not to think too hard about it.

The problem was, no one wanted to go find the panther. It wasn't that the Lost Souls weren't worried about their friend. They were just more worried about the panther eating *them*. After the meeting he'd called the previous night had ended in chaos, with everyone volunteering everyone else, Jem had decided to let them sleep on it, then make a plan first thing in the morning.

"I don't want to go any more than they do," he muttered as he scaled down the ladder. "But *someone* has to do it. And we're wasting precious time."

A few Lost Souls were already waiting in the clearing, nibbling on their breakfasts and looking as sleepless and lost as Jem felt. Sina was among them, sharpening a spear on a rock. She looked up when he arrived, but didn't smile.

"Hello," he said, and she nodded. She opened her mouth to speak, then shut it and shrugged.

"Are you all right?" he asked, and she shook her head and stuck out her tongue as if to say she felt like she might spew.

"Me too." He sighed.

She reached into the pocket of her dress and pulled out a wilted flower. Jem recognized it from the abandoned bouquet they'd found the day before. Sina bit her lip and twirled it between her fingers.

"It's okay." He put a hand on her shoulder. "We'll find him. Don't worry."

Within ten minutes, most of the crew was assembled. And most were avoiding looking Jem in the eye so he wouldn't pick them to go.

"All right," he said. "Today we're going to go to the panther's lair and save Smitty. I'm going to ask one more time for volunteers, and if no one offers, I'm just going to have to choose. And you can only volunteer *yourself*— not your mate."

But before anyone could say a thing, there was an enormous clatter over near the tree houses. The Lost Souls turned to look and gasped.

"What was that?" Edwin shrieked.

"I don't know," Jem answered, craning his neck to see. It was a noise he'd never heard before, like all kinds of wooden objects being smacked and shaken together. Like a tree house had fallen apart, or—he gasped. "The trap!"

"He's back!" screamed Ronagh. "The panther's back for more of us!"

"Is anyone still in the houses?" Edwin cried.

"I think Charlie's still there!"

"And Gil!"

Everyone began to shout at once.

"Stop!" Jem bellowed. "Everyone, calm down. We'll go back to the houses together. Follow me and stay close. The panther won't attack us if we're together." *I hope,* he added to himself.

The crew leaped into formation behind him and shuffled across the clearing like an enormous centipede.

"You're stepping on my heels!" Ronagh hissed.

"You're stepping on my toes!" Elmo retorted.

"Quiet!" said Jem. The trap was less than twenty yards away now, and he could see the coconuts and gourds still swaying. "Keep your eyes open," he told the others. "And if anyone sees him—"

"What. The. *Flotsam?*"

Jem's jaw dropped as Captain Scarlet McCray stepped out of the trees, hands on her hips.

"Scarlet!" Ronagh broke formation and ran straight for her friend.

"Wait!" Jem yelled. "What about the—"

"There *is* no panther, mate!" Tim cried. "Scarlet set off the trap!"

Relief washed over Jem, and he joined the two dozen others mobbing Scarlet with hugs.

"Stop! Stop!" Scarlet called from the middle of the crowd. "I can't breathe!"

"You came back!" Monty cried as the Lost Souls stepped back to give her some space.

"Just when we needed you!" Ronagh added, holding

on to Scarlet's waist like she might never let go.

"I had to," Scarlet began, then paused. "Wait, what do you mean, you *needed* me? You already know about Lucas?"

"We know he plans to be the most powerful pirate in the tropics," Tim said.

"Well, there's more to it than that," Scarlet reported. "He's headed this way. And Captain Wallace, too."

"What?" The crew gasped.

Scarlet nodded. "But if you didn't know that, what did you need me for?"

Jem stepped forward, head reeling. Now, on the heels of that news, he had to break the news about losing their boatswain to a big cat. "Well, it's a—"

He stopped when he spotted the girl, peeking out from behind a nearby tree.

Tim saw her, too. "Um, Cap'n . . ."

Scarlet started, as if she'd forgotten all about her. "Jo, come out," she said. "It's all right."

The girl stepped slowly out from behind her tree, wearing what must have at one time been a fine pink dress. Now it was mostly brown, and her boots were scuffed and caked with mud. She looked at the crew as if she suspected they might eat her for breakfast.

"Who's *that*?" Edwin exclaimed.

"My cousin." Scarlet reached out and pulled the girl toward her. "This is Jo."

It was obvious to Jem that the only thing keeping Jo from bolting was Scarlet's firm grip. He understood completely. He knew what it was like to feel like you were from another world. So he stepped forward and bowed to her, Old World–style. "Welcome," he said. "I'm Jem."

Jo looked surprised, but she curtsied back with a grateful smile.

"Now. Explain why you needed me," said Scarlet. "Also, what's with the ear-shattering trap?" She gestured at the noisemakers still swaying in the trees.

"Well," said Jem, "that's a panther trap, meant to scare him off. And we need you because . . ." He took a deep breath. "Because the panther got Smitty."

"Smitty?" Scarlet clapped her hands over her mouth. "The panther ate Smitty?"

"No! No!" Jem held up his hands. "Well . . . we don't think so, anyway. We think he's just . . . keeping him." He stole a glance at Jo, who looked like she might faint.

"*Keeping him?*" Scarlet cried. "What for?"

"Maybe for company?" Edwin suggested.

"Or maybe to eat later?" Ronagh whispered.

"Sink me. This is worse than I thought." Scarlet paused and chewed on her lip. "And yet, we have to go that way, anyway."

"We do? Why?" asked Tim.

"Lucas wants a panther as a pet, and he's coming for this one. Today."

"What?" Jem couldn't believe his ears.

"That's not all," Scarlet went on. "Captain Wallace is mad for revenge, so he's on his way, too. He wants to trap Lucas in the panther's lair to get rid of him."

"*What?*" Now it was Jem's turn to feel like he might faint.

Everyone began to shout again.

"*Quiet!*" Scarlet bellowed. Her cousin flinched.

"Okay." Jem took a deep breath. "So we need to go to the panther."

Scarlet nodded. "But we've also got to go to the pirates. We'll split into two crews, and both will start out right away."

"Sign me up for the pirates!" Tim called.

"Me too!" added Liam.

"Pirates for me!"

Jem shook his head. Even in the face of their captain, no one wanted to go to the panther. "All right, I'll—" he began.

"I'll go to the panther," Jo spoke up.

Every single Lost Soul turned to look at her.

Scarlet looked confused. "Sorry?"

"I'll go to the panther," Jo repeated.

Scarlet shook her head. "Uh-uh. No way. Absolutely not. I'm already going to have to explain to your father why we ran away, captained a ship, trekked through a jungle, and ruined your dress."

"I don't care about my—" Jo began.

"I'm *not* going to explain to him why you got mauled by a panther, too," said Scarlet.

Jo pulled herself up a bit taller and set her jaw. "You should let me go," she said calmly. "You know I'm a cat person."

Jem looked from Jo to Scarlet, incredulous. Obviously,

stubbornness ran in the family.

"A panther is not a house cat!" Scarlet cried.

But Jo just nodded. "I know. Trust me." She gave Scarlet a long look.

Scarlet opened her mouth to argue, then closed it and stared at Jo for a few moments. "Sina?" She turned to the older girl, who was looking at Jo the way Uncle Finn looked at his specimens.

Slowly, Sina began to nod.

Scarlet closed her eyes. "I can't believe I'm about to agree to this."

A few Lost Souls gasped.

"But," she continued, "I am. You can go to the panther, Jo. But you're not going alone."

"I'll go with her," said Jem, feeling suddenly braver now that he knew he wouldn't be alone.

"Thank you," whispered Jo.

"Thanks, Fitz," Scarlet said. "You and Jo can set off right away. I'll take this group with me to head off the pirates." She pointed to about ten Lost Souls, including Tim and Liam. "The rest of you will stay here with Sina and guard the treasure. Remember, both Lucas and Captain Wallace know exactly where it is. If they're on the island, we can't leave it alone."

"Aye-aye, Captain!" Ronagh yelled.

Scarlet stuck out her fist, and the others pressed in to pile their fists on top of hers.

"No prey, no pay, mateys," said Scarlet.

"No prey, no pay!" the Lost Souls chorused, and even Jo joined in.

"And may you die peacefully rather than in the jaws of a big bloodthirsty cat!"

Thanks, Captain. Jem rolled his eyes.

"Die peacefully!" the pirates chorused.

"We won't," Jo whispered to him.

CHAPTER FIFTEEN

They dashed through the jungle, Jem out in front, Jo close behind. She was obviously completely out of her element, tripping over roots and jumping at the sight of snakes slithering across the path. And yet she never complained, and she picked herself up without a fuss when she fell. She didn't even seem tired, although Jem doubted she'd slept much the night before.

Could she really have arrived from the Old World only the week before?

"Apparently the tropics do strange things to a person," Jo said, puffing.

Jem had to laugh. How had she known what he was thinking? He chalked it up to an Old World thing and agreed with her wholeheartedly.

When they reached the Valley of Simmering Streams, they slowed to a brisk walk. It was now midday, so Jem pulled some linty nuts out of his pocket and shared them with Jo.

"Best I've got for lunch," he said apologetically.

"It's perfect." Jo practically inhaled them.

Jem shook his head. "Perfect would be fruitcake. Or shortbread. I haven't had either of those in months."

Jo considered this and agreed. "I'd probably miss those, too, if I had to go without them. I might also miss clean clothes." She looked down at her dress and traced a streak of mud from her waist to her hem.

"Exactly!" Jem said. "And square meals. And books. Even school, sometimes." Finally, he had someone who understood where he was coming from.

"True," said Jo. "But then . . . you have all this." She spread her arms wide, taking in the valley. A pair of aras swooped and swerved overhead, squawking down at them as a warm breeze wrapped them in spices and sunshine.

Jem looked around at the valley and the jungle beyond, and felt suddenly guilty. Jo was right. He'd been envying Scarlet in her father's house in port when there were so many amazing things to be thankful for here on the island.

He made a mental list of them as they pressed on. There were the aras, the most beautiful and clever birds he'd ever known. And the monkeys, even if they were troublemakers. There were fireflies to light the night. And the feeling of waking up in a hammock in a tree house, listening to the strange trills and whistles of a hundred tropical birds. And the crew, of course—what would life be like without Tim and Liam and Smitty? And Scarlet was one of the most fascinating people he'd met in his life, hands down.

Yes, he decided. *All this is amazing. And worth protecting.*

"How much farther?" Jo wanted to know.

Jem pulled his map out of his trouser pocket. "We're about halfway. From here, we have to go south a bit." He dug his compass out of another pocket and consulted its needle. "This way." He pointed, and they began to jog again.

"What does the panther's lair look like?" Jo wanted to know.

"I'm not sure," Jem had to admit. "I've never seen it before. I've never seen the panther, either," he added, and his stomach tightened at the thought of the creature they were going to confront. He stole a glance at Jo, who looked strangely calm. "You aren't scared?" he asked.

She shook her head. "Maybe I should be, but I'm not. I like cats."

Jem raised an eyebrow. "This isn't just any cat."

"I know. But . . . I've always admired them. They're unpredictable, you know? Just when you think they're going to lie by the fire all day, they find a mouse to chase, and all of a sudden, they're wild and independent." Jo smiled. "Under the right circumstances, they rise to the occasion."

"I see," Jem said, studying the girl who'd probably spent many an hour knitting in front of a fire and was now running across a tropical island in search of a wild beast. "Still, I have no idea what we're going to do when we get there. I can't imagine how we're going to convince the panther to let Smitty go."

"I'll think of something," Jo promised, and they picked up the pace.

Soon the ground grew rockier and hillier, and the sun began to beat down on their heads. Before long, they found themselves climbing up a small mountain, then skidding down the other side into a narrow valley with a creek running through it.

They stopped briefly to refill Jem's canteen, then ran along the creek bank. Jem listened to its quiet gurgling, and for the tiniest moment he was actually able to convince himself that they were just on a nice nature walk and not a quest to confront a deadly predator.

That came to an end when Jo suddenly stopped and knelt down in the dirt.

"Look," she said, pointing at something before her.

Jem's stomach twisted. He knew what it was even before he saw it. A big panther paw print.

"Its paws are enormous," Jo breathed. "Just imagine the size of its claws!"

"Let's keep going," Jem said, not wanting to think about it.

Jo stood and shaded her eyes from the sun, surveying the small mountains on either side of them. "Look!" she said, pointing off to the right. "Is that . . . ?"

Jem followed her finger to a rocky ledge jutting out of the mountainside. Behind it, there appeared to be a gap in the rock that looked like it might be a cave. Or a lair. His stomach twisted tighter.

Jo lowered her finger. "I think we're here."

"Right." He swallowed hard. "Well, at least there's no sign of the pirates."

Jo nodded, then picked up her skirt and jogged off toward the hill. Jem had no choice but to follow.

They stopped under the ledge. "You're sure you want to go up there?" he asked.

Jo nodded. "Give me a boost."

He complied, and she helped him up after her. Soon they were both standing outside the mouth of the cave.

"We should be quiet," she whispered.

Jem nodded. His mouth was so parched he couldn't have made a sound even if he wanted to.

"His name is Smitty, right?" Jo asked, and Jem nodded again.

She crept toward the hole in the rock. "Smitty!" she whispered into it.

There was no answer.

"Smitty?"

Again, nothing.

Jo straightened. "I think it's a big cave, but it's too dark to see inside."

Jem racked his brain for a logical next step. Could they entice the panther outside? And with what?

"Are you all right?" Jo whispered.

"Me?" Jem croaked, finally finding his voice. "I'm fine."

"It's just . . . you're breathing so heavily."

"No, I'm not." He turned to look at her.

Suddenly her hand shot out and grabbed his wrist. He froze, and that's when he heard it.

Some very heavy breathing.

Just over their shoulders.

Jo dug her nails into Jem's wrist, but he was too terrified to even make a squeak.

Slowly, they turned around to find themselves face-to-face with a great big snarling black panther.

CHAPTER SIXTEEN

Scarlet led her team back to the Valley of Simmering Streams and stopped for a quick meeting.

"All right, crew," she said. "I'm not sure when the pirates will pass through here—hopefully they haven't already." She thought about Jem and Jo, and wondered if they'd encountered Captain Wallace on their way to the panther's lair. She still couldn't believe she'd sent her Old World cousin off to face a jungle cat.

"Anyway." She pulled herself back into the present. "This isn't a bad place for us to wait. The pirates will have to cross this valley on the way to the panther's lair." They had, in fact, waited in this very spot for the pirates before, just after Lucas had defected to the *Dark Ranger*.

Scarlet stared up the hill the pirates would descend and tried to imagine the ugliest, fiercest crew in the tropics appearing on top of it. She shivered. Then she shivered again to think of all the new pirates Lucas would be bringing with him. That meant that at least twice as many swabs would know about the treasure on Island X.

"We'd better hide," she said. "A few of you can take that boulder over there. And there's a big shrub that'll hide at least two. Spread out and find a spot. Then I guess all we can do is wait. I doubt they'll be long."

The Lost Souls scattered across the valley, tucking themselves under shrubs and behind giant rocks. Within a few minutes, Scarlet couldn't see anyone. She joined Tim behind a nearby boulder.

"Do you think they'll be okay?" he whispered.

"Who?"

"Jem and your cousin. I mean, neither are exactly the type to take on a panther."

Scarlet sighed. "I know. I'm not really sure what I was thinking. But something told me—"

But Scarlet never got a chance to explain, for just then, a deep voice drifted over to them. A very familiar voice. A voice that didn't belong on Island X. Scarlet thumped Tim on the shoulder, then peeked around the rock to watch Captain Wallace's crew appear atop the hill.

"This is it, Captain," Iron "Pete" Morgan announced. "Remember this valley?"

"Of course I do," Captain Wallace puffed, clambering up next to him. "And those blasted children had better not try to stop me this time. If they do, they'll be sorry."

Scarlet snorted, then stopped as two towering pirates stepped up behind him. One was missing a hand, the other an eye. Three more equally fierce-looking swabs appeared behind them. Within moments, Captain Wallace's entire crew was gathered atop the hill.

"Shivers!" Tim said.

Scarlet gulped as they thundered down into the valley. "He said he'd gather a crew to rival Lucas's, but I didn't expect this." She wouldn't have wanted to meet even one of them in a dark alley, let alone twenty.

"It's this way, Captain." A pirate with a compass

pointed south. Scarlet recognized him as one of the Blood Brothers.

But he's part of Lucas's crew, she thought. *What happened?*

"Good," said Captain Wallace. "Let's push on. There'll be no resting until that stupid child is trapped inside the panther's lair."

"We can't let them go any farther," whispered Scarlet.

"You think we can take them all?" asked Tim.

"I don't know, but we have to—"

"Stop right there!"

Scarlet froze midsentence at the sound of another familiar voice. She poked her head out again to see none other than Lucas Lawrence standing atop the hill. She thumped Tim's shoulder again. "It's Lucas!"

"Ow!" Tim rubbed his shoulder, then peered out. "Scurvy."

Lucas marched down the hill, followed by another twenty pirates with even more crooked teeth and missing fingers and battle scars than Captain Wallace's crew.

"Scurvy," she agreed.

Captain Wallace swore, and his crew gathered around him, cutlasses drawn.

"What do you think you're doing here?" Lucas yelled.

"None of your business!" Captain Wallace retorted.

"It is *too* my business!" Lucas shot back. "This is *my* island, and you're trespassing!"

Scarlet choked. She would have leaped up and run out swinging had Tim not clamped on to her arm and kept her in place.

"*Your* island!" Captain Wallace laughed. "Not likely!"

"It's as good as mine!" Lucas stabbed the air with his dagger. "And I'm telling you to leave. The crew of the *Panther* has some business to take care of."

"You'll have to get by me and my crew first!" said Captain Wallace.

Lucas laughed. "Easy! I've got the most powerful crew in all the tropics!"

"Not anymore, you don't. Remember the Blood Brothers?" Captain Wallace gestured behind him. Blake and Blair Blood gave Lucas small guilty waves.

Lucas did a double take. "What? Blair! Blake! You said you'd be on *my* crew!"

The Blood Brothers shrugged and shuffled back into the crowd.

"You'll be sorry!" Lucas shook his fist. Then he composed himself again. "Not that it matters. I've still got the meanest, ugliest crew around!"

"Hardly!" said Captain Wallace. "My men are meaner and uglier than yours. In fact, they make me sick just looking at them!" He glanced back at his men and added, "I mean that in the best possible way."

His men exchanged glances, and Pete rolled his eyes.

"Well, I've got something you don't," Lucas taunted. "Something that's going to knock your boots off. Or rather, tear them off with its big sharp teeth."

"I know about the panther," Captain Wallace said coolly.

Lucas drew back. "You do?"

"I also know you don't have it yet," Captain Wallace went on. "And I know you're not going to get it, either."

Lucas's face turned crimson. "What?" he cried. "How?"

"Because . . . ," Captain Wallace faltered, obviously realizing that he couldn't very well tell Lucas his plan.

"Because it's ours," Pete spoke up. "We're going to capture the panther ourselves."

"What?" Lucas's eyes narrowed and his nostrils flared.

"Exactly!" Captain Wallace cried. "I'm going to be the captain of the . . . the . . . the *Big Cat*!"

"That's a terrible name," Tim whispered. Pete rolled his eyes, obviously thinking the same thing.

For a moment, the two captains stared at each other. Then all at once, they both made a break for it. Lucas's men threw themselves down the mountain, and Captain Wallace's crew took off running. Scarlet ducked behind the rock and held her breath as forty pirates thundered past, elbowing and jostling and swearing at each other.

As soon as they were gone, she popped up and motioned for the other Lost Souls to do the same.

"After them!" Scarlet commanded.

They took off, about fifty yards behind the pirates. The path was now well trampled, so Scarlet could devote part of her brain to figuring out what the flotsam they were going to do when they reached the lair.

But by the time the pirates slowed, coming to a halt under a ledge that jutted out of the side of a mountain, she still hadn't come up with a good plan. So she motioned for the other Lost Souls to hide behind some nearby trees. The pirates were too busy tossing insults and spitting at each other to notice.

Lucas and Captain Wallace both pulled themselves up onto the ledge, while their crews stayed down below. Not knowing exactly what she was doing, Scarlet stepped out from the trees and marched right up to them.

"Hey!" she yelled. All eyes turned to her.

"Not again," Pete groaned.

"McCray!" Lucas's face broke into a sneer. "I was hoping you'd come. I've got plans for you, too. You and your whole crew. I'll deal with you after I finish this."

"I'd like to see you try," Scarlet retorted, although the look in his eye made her shiver again. It was the same look she'd seen in Captain Wallace's when he met with Voodoo Miranda. Lucas wanted revenge.

"This is *our* island," she told the captains, "and if you think I'm going to let any of you steal from it, you've got another thing coming!" She pulled her dagger out of her boot.

"Deadeye!" Lucas shouted, and a grizzled old sea dog with a patch over one eye stepped forward and grabbed her shoulder. She tried to pull away, but he held fast.

"All right, then." She stopped struggling and stood still, knowing full well she could take out his knees with a well-aimed kick. But as soon as she did, she'd have forty pirates down her throat, and she wasn't sure the crew was ready for that. She decided to stall. "Go on," she told them. "Get your little cat. I'll watch."

Lucas and Captain Wallace both looked surprised.

They turned toward the cave, and Lucas stepped forward, making some clucking noises.

"It's a cat, stupid, not a chicken." Captain Wallace pushed Lucas out of the way and stuck his head into the dark hole. "Hallooo?"

"Move it!" Lucas shoved him aside and peered into the cave. "Here, kitty, kitty, kitty."

A few moments later, he pulled his head out. "Nothing in there." Then he spun around to face Scarlet. "Did you take it?"

Captain Wallace began to sneak up behind Lucas, positioning himself to shove his enemy into the lair.

"You did, didn't you?" Lucas continued. "Give it back, McCray, or my men will take it from you."

All at once his entire crew was surrounding her, unsheathing their cutlasses and baring their hideous teeth. She gulped and raised her dagger, signaling to the Lost Souls that now was the time to help her.

Suddenly, Captain Wallace began shrieking and Lucas started hollering, and the men looked away from Scarlet and up at the ledge, where an enormous black panther had emerged from his lair, baring a mouthful of flesh-ripping teeth.

Scarlet froze, mouth wide open. She'd never seen anything as sleek and muscular as the panther. His head came up to Lucas's ribs, and his paws were so big they could have taken out all the pirates with a few swipes. But even more amazing, more *alarming* than the cat's rippling muscles and glimmering eyes was what was perched on his back.

It was Scarlet's cousin, Josephine.

"Sink me," Scarlet breathed.

Behind Jo, Jem was hanging on for dear life, his face as pale as the beast was black. The panther turned to glare at Lucas and Captain Wallace, who now clung to each other, trembling and babbling nonsense. Throwing back his head, he let out a roar, then leaned back on his haunches and launched himself into the air, straight for the pirate captains.

They screamed and threw themselves off the ledge, crashing into the pirates below, who were trying to scramble back the way they'd come. The panther landed lightly on the ground and paused just long enough for Jo to give Scarlet an exhilarated smile before hurtling off after the pirates.

Scarlet stood and stared after them long after they'd disappeared, trying to decide if she'd really seen her Old World cousin riding on the back of a panther and chasing the pirates off her island. Eventually, Tim joined her and tapped her shoulder.

"Captain, look." He pointed up at the ledge, where a tall, blond boy was creeping out of the den, blinking in the sunlight.

"Smitty!"

Smitty waved. "Hullo!" he called. "What's all this fuss about? I was just inside having a nice nap—a catnap, get it?" He chuckled.

"Come on, Smit," Scarlet said. "We're going home."

"Oh. Well, all right," Smitty said, clambering down from the ledge. "But you'll never believe the dream I had, just a few minutes ago. Fitz was there, with this Old World girl I'd never seen before. And somehow they tamed the panther into letting them ride him! Isn't that the craziest thing you could imagine?"

Scarlet shook her head and stared again at the path her panther-riding cousin had taken. "It doesn't get much crazier than that."

CHAPTER SEVENTEEN

"Show us again what Captain Wallace looked like!"

Tim eagerly complied, hopping to his feet and pulling Liam up with him to play the role of Lucas Lawrence. As the other Lost Souls sat around the bonfire on the edge of the clearing, Tim and Liam imitated, for the fifth time at least, Captain Wallace and Lucas babbling like babies at the sight of the black panther.

The Lost Souls howled with laughter, and Tim and Liam took their bows.

Jem leaned back on his elbows and stared up at the sky, which was now chock-full of stars. The fire warmed his bare feet, and for the first time in days, he took a deep breath and relaxed. The pirates were gone—for now, at least—and he had actually survived not only an encounter with the dreaded panther but a ride on its back.

And best of all, he would never, *ever* have to do that again.

"I want to know how Jo talked to the panther!" said Ronagh. She turned to Jo, who sat on the grass beside her. "You were amazing!"

"Oh, it was nothing, really," Jo said shyly, as all heads turned to her. She and Sina were working on a new outfit for Jo, since their adventures that day had left her dress ripped and stained. They were tearing pieces of fabric off the skirt and weaving them with long ferns to make a very different kind of dress.

"You met an enormous predator and convinced him to let us ride on his back," Jem reminded her. "I'd hardly say that's nothing."

"Did you really talk to him?" Scarlet asked from across the circle. "Like, in English?"

"I thought island animals didn't understand English," said Elmo.

"Except for the pigs," added Emmett. "But that's because they're from the Old World."

Jo shook her head. "I did talk to him. But . . ." She paused, as if trying to decide how to explain it. All the Lost Souls leaned forward expectantly. "But it's more than that. Cats need to be approached in a certain way. They need a special touch."

"So do monkeys," Ronagh said, petting the one that was sitting in her lap, snacking on some flies.

"Ships too," added Tim.

Jem looked back up at the stars, recalling how he and Jo had stood together, knees knocking, while the panther looked them up and down, as if trying to decide which one he ought to devour first. He began to pace, his enormous black muscles rippling with every step.

The highlights of Jem's life had just begun to flash before his eyes when Jo reached into her pocket and pulled something out. She took a deep breath and stepped right up to the panther, hand outstretched.

"What are you doing?" Jem had croaked. "Get back!"

The panther had stopped pacing and swung his great

head around to stare at her. Its yellow-green eyes glinted, and Jem had been absolutely certain he'd seen the last of his new friend.

But the panther tilted its head and regarded whatever Jo had in her hand. And then, slowly, he moved forward to sniff it.

Jem held his breath.

"That's a good kitty," Jo whispered. "Take your toy."

Toy? Jem couldn't believe it. She had a cat toy in her pocket?

The panther had faltered at the sound of her voice, then slowly leaned in again. And he drew back his lips to expose a mouthful of sharp and shiny teeth, which he used to pluck the object out of her hand.

Jem's mouth fell open. It was a small gray mouse, which someone had knit by hand.

"There," Josephine said softly. "I knew you'd like it. Now, look. We're here for two reasons. First of all, we need our friend back. We believe you've seen him?"

"Jo," Jem spoke up without taking his eyes off the panther that was chewing thoughtfully on the mouse's tail. "The island wildlife doesn't understand English. Just the Islander language."

Jo had considered this, then shrugged. "Well, hopefully one cat isn't too different from another. I'll just talk to him like I talk to my own." And she proceeded to explain the entire situation to him, including the approach of some pirates who wanted to capture him.

The panther kept on chewing his new toy, but he was obviously listening. Every now and then he'd look at Jo and cock his head to the side, as if to say, "You don't say. Go on."

And then, in a move that had caused Jem's jaw to practically fall off his face, the panther suddenly dropped his mouse and took a step toward Jo. And he began to *rub his head against Jo's hand*! Soon she was petting him, and before Jem knew it, they were heading deep into the cave, where Jo had clambered up on the panther's back and pulled him up behind her.

This was hands down the strangest day of my life, Jem told the stars. *But possibly also the most fantastic. And,* he reminded himself, *it never would have happened in the Old World. So score one more for Island X.*

"I think," Jo continued, "that the panther's just misunderstood. He was lonely and wanted a friend."

"Exactly!" Smitty piped up from the other side of the circle. "The panther wasn't such bad company, though he did snore even louder than Swig." He elbowed Tim in the ribs. "I think Jo's right—he just wanted a friend, and when he saw me, he knew I was the perfect one."

Tim snorted.

"Sure," said Liam. "Whatever you say . . ." He paused, coming up with a new name. "Meriwether."

For a moment, Smitty looked startled. Then as quickly as his expression had changed, it returned to normal. He shoved his hands in his pockets and whistled a tune.

But Liam had noticed it. "Wait," he said. "That's it, isn't it?"

"What's it?" Smitty said without looking at him.

"Your name!" Liam crowed. "It's Meriwether!"

The Lost Souls gasped. All heads turned to Smitty.

"No!" Smitty protested. "It's not! That's a terrible name!"

"It is!" Liam jumped to his feet. "Admit it, Meriwether! That's your name!"

"Is it really?" yelled Monty.

"Come clean, Smitty!" Gil called.

Smitty protested a few minutes longer, then gave up, throwing his hands in the air. "Fine! You got me! My name is Meriwether Smith, and now you know why I go by Smitty!"

A cheer went up around the bonfire, and several Lost Souls who'd been trying to solve the mystery for years punched the air and slapped each other on the back. Liam began to dance a jig.

"Yeah, yeah," Smitty grumbled. "Laugh it up."

But beside him, Sina was looking pensive. "Meri . . . wether," she said, trying out the name. "Meriwether." Then she nodded and smiled.

Smitty turned to her, incredulous. "You *like* it?"

"Meriwether." Sina tried it out again. She nodded.

"Well, sure, it sounds good when *you* say it," Smitty muttered as the others hooted with laughter.

Later, as the Lost Souls began to wander off to their tree houses, Jem joined Scarlet to help douse the fire.

"It's been quite the week," she commented, pouring water from her canteen on the embers.

"That's the understatement of the century," Jem told her.

"You did well here, taking care of everyone," Scarlet said. "And that panther trap was pretty brilliant."

"Thanks," Jem said. "Too bad we didn't get to test it on a real panther."

"I wouldn't be surprised if we got to test it on some pirates someday soon." Scarlet kicked some dirt on the coals and sighed. "We sure haven't seen the last of them."

They both fell silent for a moment, pondering what Lucas and Captain Wallace might do next. Then Scarlet said, "You know, Fitz, I think you might make a good captain some day."

"Really?" Jem turned to her. "You think?" This was the highest praise he'd ever heard come out of her mouth.

She nodded. "You're a good leader."

"Wait, you're not thinking of leaving, are you? Did a week of hot breakfasts and shiny cutlery make you go soft?" He poked her in the shoulder.

She laughed. "Not on your life. I'm just thinking ahead. Even a good captain can't stay captain forever."

Captain, Jem thought to himself. *Captain Fitzgerald.* It had a nice ring to it. Maybe someday . . .

"Speaking of breakfasts and cutlery, I'm going to have to take Jo back to port tomorrow." Scarlet sighed.

"I'll come with you," he offered.

"You can watch my father feed me to the sharks."

Jem put a hand on his captain's shoulder. "Let's deal with that tomorrow," he suggested. "Right now, let's get some sleep."

174

CHAPTER EIGHTEEN

Scarlet slept more soundly than she had in ages, lulled by the jungle insect chorus. She probably would have slept right through the next day had an enormous clatter not awoken her around midmorning. She practically fell out of her hammock onto the tree house floor.

"What was that?" Jo sat up in the hammock beside hers.

"The trap!" Ronagh hopped out of her own hammock and ran to the door. "The panther's back!"

Scarlet looked at her cousin. "Really?"

Jo frowned. "I'd be surprised. After yesterday, he didn't seem to want anything to do with humans for a long time." She untangled herself from the hammock and was just helping Scarlet up off the floor when they heard a familiar voice.

"What on earth is going on?" it bellowed. "Josephine? Where are you?"

"Scurvy!" Scarlet cried as Jo's eyes widened to twice their size. "Your father!"

They ran to the door and looked out. Sure enough, four men were standing below the tree houses, trying to steady the coconut shells and hollow gourds swinging above their heads.

"And my father, too!" Scarlet croaked. It hadn't occurred to her that the men would hop on a ship and come find them, but of course it made sense. Uncle Daniel would have gone crazy upon realizing that Jo was gone. The admiral must have had no choice but to bring him to the island. But how much about it had he told him? She peered down at her uncle, remembering his search for a cure for the plague. It was an important mission, but it couldn't happen here, not on her island. She had to get him off before he discovered anything of interest.

"Uncle Finn and Thomas are back!" Ronagh said. "But what are the other two doing here?"

"Safe to assume they're going to string us up by our toes." Scarlet put a steadying hand on Jo's shoulder as her cousin moaned softly. "Come on."

She scaled down the swinging ladder and landed in front of the men. Summoning her courage, she looked up at her father. "Hello."

From his frown, she could tell he was trying very hard not to box her ears.

"Josephine!" Uncle Daniel called up to his daughter, who was climbing down the ladder. "Get down from there! You'll get hurt! And what on earth are you wearing?"

Jo hopped down onto the dirt, dressed in the outfit she and Sina had made the previous evening. Her dress looked like the one Sina wore, much lighter and easier to move in than her frilly pink frock. Jo had done a fine job, Scarlet thought. But Uncle Daniel's horrified face indicated that he didn't agree.

He swept Jo up in a hug. "Josephine, I was so worried! What on earth possessed you to run away? Look at you!

You're filthy and sunburned and . . ." He caught sight of her bare feet and cringed. "And where are your *shoes*? You'll catch your death of cold! I just can't imagine what's gotten into you!" He tossed a murderous glare at Scarlet and drew his daughter closer.

Scarlet cheeks burned, and she almost informed him that Jo was just fine, thank you. In fact, she was better than fine. She was strong and healthy and incredibly brave. But this was Jo's battle to fight, not her own. So she bit her tongue and concentrated on avoiding her own father's eyes.

"Father," Jo said, gently pushing him away, "I'm fine. I'm not cold, and I'm not sick. But I am sorry that I ran away. It's just that Scarlet's island was in danger. There were pirates invading, and we had to—"

"Pirates!" Uncle Daniel exploded. He turned to his brother. "You didn't tell me anything about pirates!"

Admiral McCray opened his mouth to speak, but Scarlet interjected. "Don't be angry with Jo," she said. "It's my fault. I don't know how much my father's told you about this place, but I'm guessing you know that it's my home, and that I have a responsibility to protect it."

Uncle Daniel turned to her. "And that . . . that just can't be true! A child, taking care of an island? It's preposterous!"

Scarlet glanced around to see most of her crew had gathered to listen in. "Not just one child," she told him. "A crew of children. The bravest and strongest children in all the tropics. And I know it must sound strange to you, but this is what we do. And we do it well. Yesterday we all banded together to chase some awful swabs off the island."

Uncle Daniel looked around at the crew. His mouth hung open, but no words came out.

"But it was my fault that Jo ended up here," Scarlet continued. "So blame me for that, but don't get angry at her."

"Or," the admiral spoke up, "you could just be proud of them both."

Scarlet drew in her breath, finally daring to look him in the eyes.

"Oh, don't think I'm not furious with you, daughter," he said. "You ran away, and you put your cousin's life in danger. But we'll deal with that later. Right now, I'm proud of you for defending your home."

Warmth filled her from head to toe.

Uncle Daniel shook his head. "I . . . I don't understand this at all," he said helplessly, turning to Jo. "All I know is that I want . . . No, I *need* for you to be safe."

She gave him a hug. "I am, I promise. I've never felt better."

The admiral cleared his throat and addressed the whole crew. "Now, I know what you're all thinking. And my brother won't tell anyone about Island X. Will you, Daniel?"

Daniel opened his mouth, then shut it. He shook his head, still looking confused. But his confusion turned to complete bewilderment when a rustle in the trees made everyone turn. Sina and Kapu emerged to join the crew and froze at the sight of the newcomer.

"Blast!" Scarlet whispered. For even if he *was* her uncle, and even if he promised not to tell anyone, she still didn't want him to know about the Islanders. It didn't feel right.

"Is that . . . ? Are they . . . ?" he whispered.

"I'll explain later," Scarlet's father told him. "Now, let's go find some food before we head back." And he steered his brother off into the clearing.

The crew clustered around Scarlet and Jo.

"Do you think we can trust him?" asked Tim.

"I hope so," said Scarlet. She glanced at Jo, who nodded.

"I'll talk to him about it. I'll make him understand," she promised.

Scarlet sighed. It wasn't satisfying—not by a long shot. But it was all she had for the moment.

Jem turned to Uncle Finn. "So, how did you all find each other?" he asked. "And how did you get back here?"

"Well." Uncle Finn folded his hands over his belly. "Thomas noticed the *Hop*'s absence first thing yesterday morning. We assumed Scarlet had taken it for one reason or another, but to be certain, we tracked down the admiral, and sure enough, she'd disappeared. That was quite the kerfuffle you two caused." He gave the girls a stern look. "But fortunately, Daniel's friend Humphries had a sloop anchored in port, so we got his permission to borrow it for a few days."

"Humphries." Scarlet shuddered at the thought of Ben's future father-in-law. At least he hadn't insisted on coming himself.

"Do you know him?" asked Uncle Finn, and Scarlet nodded. "Well then, you'll be happy to know that he's the proud owner of a brand-new head of hair."

"Dark as night and silky smooth," added Thomas.

"He was my best test subject yet," finished Uncle Finn.

Scarlet wrinkled her nose, trying to picture it. "Really?"

"So the human tests were a success?" asked Jem.

"That's an understatement," said Uncle Finn. "Port Aberhard is now simply crawling with abnormally hairy pirates! It's a thing of wonder!"

"Congratulations." Jem grinned.

"Humphries himself is actually very interested in the results. In fact, he offered to help cultivate the plants, when the time comes to sell the cure. He wants to dedicate a few acres of his plantation entirely to bromeliads. He thinks it'll be a very—"

"Lucrative business." Scarlet rolled her eyes. Of course he did.

"Well, I won't be ready to think about that for a while," said Uncle Finn. "First, I have to present my findings to the High Commission on Neotropical Plantlife." He turned to Jem and put his hands on his nephew's shoulders. "This is it, boy. The study is over. We're going home!"

Jem's mouth fell open. Scarlet's followed suit.

"Home?" Jem repeated. "To the Old World?"

"Well, the High Commission isn't going to come to us." Uncle Finn laughed. "I'm going to book our passage as soon as we get back to port. Hopefully we can ship out in the next week or so. I'll need to make sure I've got all the samples I can carry, and Thomas will have to . . ."

Uncle Finn kept prattling on about his plans, but Scarlet stopped listening.

Jem was going home.

How could she let him go home?

Jo, on the other hand, was beaming. "You'll get your books back," she said. "And that shortbread you've been wanting. And we'll get to see each other when I get back!"

"But . . . but . . . you can't go," Scarlet sputtered. "Not now. Not with Lucas and Captain Wallace out there." Her voice caught in her throat.

"Well, children," said Uncle Finn. "This is truly a once-in-a-lifetime accomplishment. And you all helped, in some way. Aren't you thrilled?"

"Thrilled," Jo said sincerely.

"I'm over the moon." Scarlet glowered.

Jem stayed quiet.

Uncle Finn nodded. "Well, I'm off to find some food. What a week this has been!" He and Thomas set off for the clearing, leaving Scarlet, Jem, and Jo standing under the noisemaker trap.

"Look, we'll figure something out," Jem said, although his voice sounded shaky. "I'm sure . . . I'm sure we can come up with a good plan."

"Right," Scarlet said, although she didn't believe him for a second. Trouble was brewing, she could just feel it.

She turned on her heel and marched off into the jungle.

GLOSSARY

Amulet: an object worn, often as a piece of jewelry around the neck, to ward off evil

Blimey: an expression of frustration or surprise as in, "Remember when you dropped the anchor on my foot? Blimey, that hurt!"

Broadsword: a large, heavy sword with a broad blade

Buccaneer: a pirate. The term *buccaneer* comes from a French word (*boucanier*) which means "barbecuer." In the 1600s, buccaneers were humble men who sold barbecued meats to sailors passing through ports. Eventually they realized the opportunity passing them by and gave up their grills to make their fortunes by pillaging and plundering.

Careen: to lean a ship on one side for cleaning or repairing

Castaway: a person lucky enough to survive a shipwreck and wash ashore, hopefully not on the Island of Smelly Wild Pigs

Crow's nest: the lookout platform near the top of a mast, not the best place for pirates afraid of heights

Cutlass: a short, curved sword with a single cutting edge, a pirate's best friend

Doubloon: a Spanish gold coin, similar to the chocolate variety, but less tasty

Drivelswigger: a pirate who spends too much time reading about all things nautical

Flotsam: floating debris or rubbish

Fo'c'sle: the raised part of the upper deck at the front of a ship, also called the forecastle

Gun deck: the deck on which the ship's cannons are carried

Jack-tar: a sailor

Keelhaul: the worst possible punishment on board a ship. The offender's hands are bound to a rope that runs underneath the ship, and he is thrown overboard and dragged from one end to the other.

Long drop: the Lost Souls' own term for the toilet

Mast: a long pole that rises from the ship's deck and supports the sails

Piece of eight: a Spanish silver coin

Plank: the piece of wood that hangs off the side of the ship, like a soon-to-be-dead-man's diving board. Unlucky sailors must walk it to their doom.

Plunder: to steal, or an act of thievery

Poop deck: the highest deck at the stern of a ship. It has nothing to do with the long drop, by the way.

Port: a sailor's word for *left*

Quarterdeck: the rear part of the upper deck at the front of a ship

Quartermaster: usually the second-in-command on a ship

Scalawag: a rascal, rogue, scoundrel, or general mischief-maker

Schooner: a ship with two or more masts. One explanation suggests that the name comes from the Scottish term "to scoon," which means "to skim upon the surface."

Scuttle: a word used by the Lost Souls to describe something awful as in, "Hardtack for breakfast again? That scuttles!"

Sloop: a small, single-mast ship

Spyglass: a much more intriguing name for a small telescope

Starboard: a sailor's word for *right*

Swain: a short form of *boatswain,* meaning a sailor of the lowest rank, more of a servant

The Hop's
hiding spot

Ara
Rookery

X Lost Souls
camp

Ophidian's
Aggregation

N
W   E
S

Island X

ACKNOWLEDGMENTS

First, to the Inkslingers: Tanya Kyi, Kallie George, Christy Goerzen, Maryn Quarless, and Lori Sherritt-Fleming. I hope that every author, at some point, has a crazy-talented group of colleagues and friends they can count on for apt feedback, moral support, and quality baked goods. Thank you all so much.

Thanks to Pamela Bobowicz for her patience and wise words as well as the entire team at Grosset & Dunlap. Thanks to my agent, Marie Campbell, for tirelessly championing the Lost Souls, and to the talented Gerald Guerlais for the wonderful cover art.

And, always, to Louise Delaney, who continues to perform incredible feats in the name of her daughter's writing career, most recently enduring severe frostbite in the dead of winter in Russia. I am one lucky, lucky girl.

ABOUT THE AUTHOR

Rachelle Delaney lives in Vancouver, Canada, where she works as a writer, editor, and creative writing teacher. In 2010 she was named the top emerging writer in Canada by the Canadian Author's Association.

Relive the adventure from the beginning!

THE SHIP
of
LOST SOULS

1

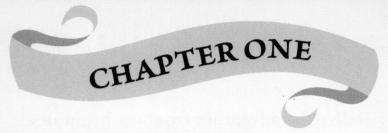

CHAPTER ONE

"You there! Get away from that!"

Scarlet McCray had known the crime could land her in deep trouble. For an instant, she'd even considered not going through with it. But then, she'd never been one to let consequences stop her from wreaking havoc, even if the consequences included having one's limbs lopped off. So why, she'd reasoned, start now?

This time, however, after the deed was done and she found herself staring into a merchant's bloodshot eyes of rage, it occurred to her that she might have gone too far.

"Why you . . . you'll pay for that!"

Not that she regretted it. Not one bit. No, this just meant she'd have to run faster.

"Blasted little scalawag. I'll tear you limb from—"

Scarlet didn't stick around to hear the plan. With an innocent shrug and a tip of her cap, she took off sprinting through the streets of Port Aberhard. A hand reached out to stop her, but she twisted and slipped to the left. A King's Man moved to block her path, but she ducked out of his reach and ran on, dodging a pack of pirates and hurdling a barrel of rum, pumping her arms as the thud of her heart began to drown out the voices of her pursuers. She knew this routine well and was content to let the port town blur into shapes and smells, light and shadows. She liked it better that way.

Scarlet McCray could find her way around Port Aberhard bound and blindfolded. She knew it as well as she knew her own worn boots, her crew, and the ship they called home. Port Aberhard looked the same, smelled the same, and felt the same as all the other port towns on all the other islands. Its red dirt roads teemed with ruddy merchants reeking of pipe smoke, loudmouthed pirates drawn to the tavern like compass needles to magnetic north, and King's Men sweltering under blue wool coats, their brass buttons winking under a tropical sun. Smells of fried conch, sweet seaweed, and sour rum clung to the humid air, mingling with the scent of spices from inland forests.

The port towns even sounded the same—grumbling pirates, clipped orders from King's Men, and gleeful cries from cabin boys on leave from the ships they worked on.

But most important was the feeling a person got walking through the ports all over the islands. It was an unnatural feeling. A downright unsettling feeling. The pirates blamed it on the spirits of the Islanders, a people killed by the King's Men in their hunt for treasure. The King's Men declared it to be the feeling of untamed wilderness. Others called it dark magic. Voodoo. No one could agree on exactly what caused this feeling, but neither could they deny its existence. And some islands had it worse than others. Much, much worse.

Scarlet herself had long ago stopped trying to find an explanation for the chill that made her toes curl and her ears tingle every time her crew docked in port. But it never left her—especially not when she was running for her life.

She'd just glanced over her shoulder to see how far she'd outrun the merchant when a sudden wind swept in from the docks and lifted the cap off her head, sending her tangled black hair tumbling down her back. "Scurvy!" Scarlet cried, flailing her arms in an attempt to catch her cap. But it rolled over her shoulder and along the road. "Not now!" She did an about-face, ducked low to snatch it up, and kept running. Leaving the cap behind wasn't an option, for where would she be without her disguise? In a boatload of trouble, that's where.

Soon she came upon a suitably dank and shadowy alley and dove inside. She found a decent hiding spot behind a mound of old crates and crouched there, hugging her knees, hoping the merchant and his helpers hadn't closed in when she'd nearly blown her cover. If they found her, they'd turn her in to the King's Men for punishment. And supposing they discovered that the skinny, dark-eyed boy in ragged trousers and an old gray coat was actually a twelve-year-old girl? That would absolutely scuttle.

Anyway, hers had been a valiant crime as far as crimes went. She'd do it again in an instant, no hesitation. Just fifteen minutes ago she'd been slinking along between the docks, looking for a shiny, green lime or a stray doubloon to pocket, when she spotted a merchant with a great big cage full of birds. Having always been partial to winged things, she approached and instantly felt her stomach turn when she realized what kind of birds the merchant was selling. Only one island creature had such beautiful, ruby-red feathers, marked by a single band of blue and green on each wing.

The Islanders had called them "aras." They'd nearly been killed off completely a few decades ago when the King's Men first invaded the islands to harvest exotic wood and spices and send them back to greedy King Aberhard. The birds' beauty had been their undoing. As soon as the King's Men arrived, they began to blast them out of the sky, then ship their red feathers back to the Old World in overstuffed canvas sacks. Rumor had it that every night, King Aberhard rested his big, greasy head on a pillow stuffed with ara feathers. The thought made Scarlet's blood simmer.

But that wasn't even the worst of it. Old Worlders of all kinds, from spice merchants and wood cutters to plantation owners and pirates, soon descended on the islands as well, hoping to get in on the pillaging and plundering, especially if it unearthed a bounty of precious jewels. The native Islanders, who'd lived in leafy huts and tended garden plots on the islands for hundreds of years, watched with increasing alarm as these pale, brisk men invaded their homelands and spread Old World diseases among them. Islander numbers fell as hard and as fast as the trees around them, and one particularly deadly plague, known as the Island Fever, was rumored to have killed them off completely.

Scarlet hated that story. It made her stomach ache just as badly as the story of the aras. For perhaps the thousandth time, she wished she could have done something to save them.

And so, when she saw the merchant's cage nearly overflowing with the rare red birds, Scarlet wasted no time in committing her crime of passion. She marched right up, grasped the doors of the cage with both hands, and yanked them wide open.

The aras needed no instructions. Out the doors they flew, a long, red ribbon streaking across the sky toward the jungle and hopefully home.

Home. Scarlet bit her lip as she watched them, and for a moment she forgot that she was a criminal, being sized up by a seething merchant with bloodshot eyes and bared teeth . . .

"Stop the boy!"

Tucked away in her hiding spot, Scarlet heard the merchant and a few other men run past, boots crunching on gravel. She let her breath out in a whoosh, then grinned. She'd saved some powerless creatures and made life a little more difficult for the gluttonous, overdressed Old Worlders. Wishing every day could feel so productive, she stood up and dusted off her grimy trousers. Now she'd just sneak out, find her crew, and regale them with the tale of her daring adventure. Maybe it would inspire them in their own mission. They were, after all, in dire need of inspiration.

She stepped out of the alley, blinked in the sunlight, and headed back toward the docks, pulling her cap down low over her eyes, just in case.

A new ship had docked in port—a great big schooner

with Old World flags quivering in the silver afternoon sky. Passengers stumbled from its deck to the dock, looking stunned and grateful to have both feet on firm ground. Most were King's Men, smoothing the wrinkles in their coats and trousers. But two of the travelers, neither one in uniform, stood out against the crowd. One—middle-aged and fat with a shiny scalp—studied a compass. But it was his companion who drew Scarlet's attention: a smallish boy around her age, staring slack-jawed at the busy port before him.

She knew right away what had brought them there. These days, sailors lay anchor in the islands for one reason alone: to search for treasure. Around the time the Island Fever had begun to rage—some seven or eight years ago—one of King Aberhard's underlings began to speak of a treasure he'd come upon. Unfortunately, the man—Admiral Something-or-Other—perished of the fever himself before he got around to explaining exactly what the treasure entailed. But he had captured the curiosity of the king, who promised a hefty reward to whoever found the mysterious thing. Even now, years later, boatloads of pirates, merchants, and King's Men flocked to the tropics, practically drooling at the notion of unearthing the treasure. Most even enjoyed the mystery surrounding it—at first, anyway.

Scarlet studied the boy, noting his tailored coat and stiff, shiny boots. His companion's clothes were slightly more weathered. She wondered how the boy would fare in this part of the world. The islands, rife with drunkards and thieves and generally unsavory types, didn't exactly cater to children and their notion of fun.

Maybe . . . she squinted at the sun, still high overhead. She had a good hour before she had to meet her crew. She could follow these two, just for a bit, to find out what they were about. Children didn't arrive in port every day, and Scarlet knew it was her duty to check this one out.

The boy's traveling companion, maybe his father or some other relative, was pointing to the tavern and patting his protruding belly. Hungry, of course; they'd probably eaten little but hardtack since leaving the Old World. And judging by their tailored coats and stiff, shiny boots, they were more accustomed to dining on roast duck and buttery pastries than gnawing on the rock-hard biscuits that passed as dinner on board a ship. The boy was smoothing down his sandy-brown hair and adjusting his cuffs as if the tavern might have a dress code. Scarlet snickered. The only clothing requirement in port was a sturdy pair of boots, spacious enough to house at least one dagger.

She waited a moment after the pair marched into the tavern, then slipped inside herself. One good thing about the port towns was that the pirates and King's Men who inhabited them were so busy eyeing one another, hoping to catch the other in some wrongdoing, that they didn't notice much else. They rarely noticed stray children wandering around. Unless, of course, those stray children let themselves get spotted while, say, releasing animals in danger of extinction. Scarlet reminded herself to keep a lookout for the merchant with the bloodshot eyes.

The boy and his companion claimed two rickety

wooden chairs on either side of a table sticky with rum, and the boy, looking ravenous, stared around him, eyes unblinking. Scarlet scanned the dim room, barely half full of sailors at this time of day, and slunk along the wall to a dark little nook not far from their table where she could stand for a while without being noticed. The tavern owner gave the newcomers' well-dressed figures a once-over, then hurried into the back with promises of fresh fish.

"After a good meal," the older man was saying, "we'll reconvene in our boarding house and discuss plans for tomorrow." He spoke with an educated accent and an air of authority that Scarlet decided would drive her mad after a day or two. "I'm going to ask Captain Noseworthy about hiring a small sloop to take us there. We'll have to find a few trusty shipmates to join us for navigational purposes—men who won't take off with the . . ." He lowered his voice. "The you-know-what."

Scarlet leaned toward them. She'd bet her front teeth she knew what! But everyone and his monkey had a theory about where the treasure was hidden. Could these two really know any better? She listened closely.

"Do you think," the boy said as he tried to find a clean spot on the table to settle his elbows, "that these men are real pirates, or do you think they just read the stories and dress up like them?"

The older man shushed him, and Scarlet stifled a guffaw. Real pirates? This one had obviously never set foot off the Old World. No wonder his eyes were so wide.

"Quiet, Jem. Don't say anything that might get you stabbed. Now look, I think it would be most useful if tonight you reviewed the botany journals I gave you. You're going to need to identify everything from *Mondatricus triceriaptus* to—"

"Yes, Uncle Finn," the boy named Jem said with a little groan, as if he'd heard this a hundred times before. Scarlet frowned. She wouldn't know a *Mondatricus triceriaptus* if one tripped her and sat on her. Nor did she know what it had to do with the treasure. "But I'd much rather—"

Just then, their fish arrived, and the two tucked in, barely surfacing for air as they devoured every morsel on their plates in concentrated silence. Once finished, they paid and stood to leave. Scarlet followed, for she, too, had business to get back to.

Outside, she trailed Jem and his uncle until they rounded the next corner and stepped into another dim alley, at the end of which stood a ramshackle boarding house. Scarlet was about to let them go on their way when she saw a strange sight: a shadow—no, two shadows—pressed up against the alley wall, frozen and silent, waiting. This didn't look good. Shadows in a dark alley almost always meant bad news. Scarlet was about to call out a warning when a hand clamped down on her shoulder and spun her around, knocking off her cap. "Gotcha!" a gruff voice proclaimed, and she found herself face-to-face once again with her favorite merchant.

The man started at the sight of her long, dark hair. For a moment he softened his grip on her shoulder, as if unsure what to do. Then he seemed to remember something—probably the sight of the aras streaking across the sky—and he dug his tobacco-stained fingers into her skin again. "So the little thief's a girl, is he?" The merchant shook his head and sneered.

Scarlet squirmed under his grip. "Um, *she*," she said, scanning the alley for an escape route as best she could without making it too obvious.

"Heh?" The fury faded from the merchant's eyes, replaced momentarily with uncertainty.

"She," Scarlet repeated, buying herself some more time. "You said, 'So the little thief's a girl, is he?' And that would make *he* a *she*. See?" There was a big stick nearby—if she could just reach it, maybe she could pound him senseless.

"Oh."

"Hm. Pronouns. Tricky things." Ah. A ladder. Even better. It seemed to reach up to the rooftop of the building on her left.

"Er. I . . ." The merchant now looked thoroughly confused.

"Right. Think about that for a while." With a few swift motions, Scarlet squirmed out of the man's grasp, stomped on his right foot, booted his left shin, and made a dive for the ladder as he keeled over, swearing. She scaled the rungs like a monkey, pulled herself up onto the roof, then ran to another edge so she could look down on the alley where she'd last seen Jem and his uncle.

They'd disappeared and so had the two mysterious shadows. Scarlet ran farther along the edge of the roof and saw several figures ducking down another lane. Two of them seemed to be struggling, accompanied by the unmistakable clang of pirate cutlasses.

"Scurvy!" Scarlet cried, for now it was too late to help them. If only she'd been quicker or more aware of that blasted merchant's whereabouts. *Jem must be terrified,* she thought. He was, after all, only a child, unused to the dangers of . . .

Scarlet paused for a moment, then snapped her fingers and laughed out loud. A child in need of help. Right here on the islands. She couldn't have planned it better herself! It was exactly what her crew needed.

But now she was wasting precious seconds. She scanned the scene below her until she found the pirates and their prey and watched until she was fairly certain she knew which ship was theirs. Then she drew a breath and ran straight to the edge of the rooftop. She leaped across the gap to the next building, which she knew had a rain gutter, for she'd shimmied up and down it before during port raids. She put two fingers to her lips and let out one shrill blast, then another. The signal. Her crew would meet her at the ship, hopefully right away. There was no time to lose.

The Lost Souls' adventure continues!

THE SHIP of LOST SOULS

THE GUARDIANS of ISLAND X

2

CHAPTER ONE

Scarlet McCray was beginning to regret going barefoot. At the time, it had seemed like a jolly idea. After all, her feet hadn't even known a stocking for the first five years of her life. So why, she'd reasoned, confine her toes to some rat-eaten boots now that she was back in the place of her birth?

Except that now as she crept through the jungle, twigs snapping under her heels and burrs burrowing between her toes, she suspected she'd been too hasty in handing them off to that monkey who'd eyed them hopefully.

Maybe it was the funny kink in his long black tail. Or the way his fur stood up on one side of his head, like he'd just rolled out of bed. Whatever it was, Scarlet had been charmed into trusting him.

"But look, Monkey," she'd said as she tugged the boots off her feet, "you've got to take good care of these. I'll need them next time we set off on the *Hop* for a supply run."

The monkey had responded by snatching up the boots, pinching his nose, and scampering off, leaving Scarlet to wonder if she'd ever actually see them again.

She pushed aside a massive fern and climbed over a rock nearly as big as herself. Then she stopped to concentrate. At first she felt nothing, but after a few moments . . . yes, there it was. A faint tremor. And if she stood perfectly still and squeezed her eyes shut, she could feel something else. Uncertainty. Panic. Somewhere on the island, there were animals in distress. And it was up to her to find them.

Unfortunately, in a place like Island X, so full of surprises, this was no easy job.

It had only been a month since Scarlet and her crew had first set foot on the X-shaped island, but in that time she'd made more amazing discoveries than she had in her entire life. To start, she'd realized that Island X was, in fact, her birthplace. Scarlet was part Islander—one of the only remaining members of a culture killed off when people from the Old World came to the islands, bringing diseases and despair. Perhaps even the *only* remaining member.

And if that weren't overwhelming enough, she'd also discovered that somehow she was able to channel the island's animals and feel what they were feeling. If a flock of parrots rejoiced in the fruit of a nearby tree, her heart felt light and joyful. If the chief of the local band of smelly wild pigs had slept badly the night before, she felt that, too. It was a huge honor, an amazing ability. Not to mention totally perplexing.

The problem was, she could never tell when an animal in distress needed her help. Just an hour ago, for example, she'd followed a panicky feeling to its source, only to find the monkey with the kink in his tail having a temper tantrum because his brother had stolen his breakfast of termites. (He quickly got over it when she agreed to lend him her boots.)

Then, as soon as he'd left, she'd channeled another upset feeling. This one, she was fairly certain, came from the aras, her very favorite kind of bird. And while it was possible the aras were simply being harassed by hummingbirds, it was also possible that they were trying to warn her of something far more important. Like, for instance, a troop of treasure-hungry pirates. So she had no choice but to search for them—which was what she was doing now.

"If only I knew where I was," Scarlet grumbled, looking around the jungle with her fists on her hips. She concentrated hard. It was like a game of Hot and Cold, which the Lost Souls sometimes played on board the *Margaret's Hop*. Someone would hide a "treasure"— usually a lime or a piece of hardtack—while someone else would get blindfolded. Then the crew would yell "Hotttt!" or "Cooold!" as the blind one wandered toward or away from the treasure. In Scarlet's case, though, the feeling of distress grew stronger the closer she came to the anxious animal.

It felt strongest over to her left, but as she took a step in that direction, her foot sank right into a patch of amber-colored mud. "Blasted boots," she growled as the mud oozed between her toes. "And blasted monkey."

Trying to ignore her mucky foot, she inched toward some soft, leafy shrubs. "Maybe if I just cut through here . . ." Scarlet slipped between the shrubs, pushed through a wall of ferns, and found herself standing underneath the trees that held the aras' nests. Exactly where she wanted to be.

"But how . . . ?" She looked up into the tree branches and sighed. Her new talent was just one of many things about this island that she didn't understand. Its geography was another. Not for the first time, she wished her crew's only map hadn't been stolen by the treasure-hungry pirates. But then, she reminded herself for what must have been the millionth time since they'd landed on the island, what kind of Islander needs a map?

"An Islander who was forced to forget all about her island, that's who," she muttered.

When Scarlet was five years old, the Island Fever had struck her village, and her Islander mother had fallen ill. She'd begged her husband, a former admiral for the King's Men, to take Scarlet off the island and keep her healthy. Scarlet never saw her mother again.

Her father, John McCray, had returned to the King's Men, leaving Scarlet with a governess named Mary Lewis (aka Scary Mary), who'd made every attempt to erase Scarlet's memories of her old life. She'd even forced her to do awful things like curl her hair and wear petticoats and learn English.

Not that the English lessons themselves were awful. It was being forced to forget her language that truly scuttled. Now, with no other Islanders around, Scarlet doubted it would ever come back to her.

She studied the tree branches above her until she spotted a sparkle of red. Then she concentrated hard. The aras' distress was gone.

"Figures."

Scarlet grasped a low branch and swung herself up

into the nearest tree. She could climb it blindfolded by now. High above the ground, she settled into her usual spot on a sturdy branch and looked around. To her left she could see the clearing where the Lost Souls were camped. To her right stood another tree and another beyond it. And in those trees sat dozens of birds' nests—a rookery, the Old Worlders called it. And in those birds' nests sat dozens of sleepy scarlet-red birds with bands of green and blue on their wings. The aras. They didn't look a bit distressed.

"Well?" she said. "What was all that fuss about? Hummingbirds? Rotten fruit? Come on, I came all this way for *nothing*?"

A few aras eyed her drowsily, fluffed up their feathers, and went back to sleep.

"Honestly." Another problem, as she'd recently discovered, was that while she could understand what the animals were feeling, she had no way to communicate with them. No matter how much time Scarlet spent with them, the aras never seemed to understand a word she said.

A beam of sunlight sneaked through the tree canopy, illuminating specks of red in each nest, and despite her annoyance Scarlet couldn't help but smile. All these years, the King's Men and the pirates had been scouring the islands for treasure, as well as wood and spices, but they'd rarely come across a single jewel. Perhaps because the aras hid them so well. The birds simply scraped the ground with their beaks, nabbed the rubies here and there, and tucked them into the walls of their nests for safekeeping.

The King's Men, meanwhile, continued hunting the aras to near extinction for their gorgeous red feathers, not realizing that the birds were the key to the treasure they so desperately searched for.

Scarlet leaned back against the tree trunk and sighed. It was a funny situation, but not laugh-out-loud funny. The kind of funny that made you want to spit.

She turned away from the birds to look down on the Lost Souls' camp. It wasn't the place she'd originally called home; she had yet to find the spot where the Islanders' village once stood, although she guessed it was about an hour's journey from here. This clearing, with its long, soft grass and glistening freshwater pool, was a special place the Islanders used to visit a few times a year to relax, chat with neighbors, and harvest food and spices. It had a safe and peaceful feeling about it, which lingered even now, years after the last Islanders had been here. Scarlet was fairly certain they were still here in spirit, though. Island X was rumored to be one of *those* islands, filled with spirits and spooks that kept the pirates and King's Men far from its shores. Scarlet believed it was just the Islanders continuing to protect their home.

If she concentrated hard enough, she could picture the clearing as it had looked years ago—with children playing tag around the pool while their parents talked and filled baskets with seeds to grind into spices. If she focused even harder, she could picture her mother among them, tall and graceful and beautiful. And if she was very lucky, she could make out her father. Strong and relaxed and happy.

In a way, she'd not only lost her mother when the Island Fever hit, but her father, too. At least the father she knew and loved.

Once they'd left Island X, he rarely even paid her and Scary Mary a visit at the house where they lived in Jamestown. When he did, he was stern and stony. He refused to talk about the past and their life in the village or to call his daughter by her true name, Ara, which meant both a fiery shade of red and the brilliant bird of the same color.

Scarlet hadn't seen her father in nearly three years now, not since he'd announced that he was sending her to live with his family in the Old World. While Scarlet had been thrilled at the thought of escaping Scary Mary, she'd had no intention of spending the rest of her life in Old World ribbons and petticoats. So one afternoon, she'd up and run away. And it was a good thing, too, because if she hadn't, she'd never have met up with the Lost Souls or joined their jolly ship *or* been named their captain.

She squinted at the clearing. She could make out a few of the figures below: Liam and Ronagh Flannigan were playing catch with an enormous mushroom while Tim Sanders, the quartermaster of the *Margaret's Hop*, sat cross-legged near the pool, reading a thick book he'd lugged up from the ship. Other Lost Souls played Smelly Wild Pig in the Middle on the grass, and still more swung upside down in a nearby tree, screeching like monkeys.

From afar, Scarlet thought, they looked like normal Lost Souls. But she knew better. Her crew had been acting a little off since she'd made the "new mission" announcement a few weeks back. She felt their uncertainty as clearly as she'd felt the aras' anxiety or the monkey's outrage over his stolen breakfast.

It wasn't that the Lost Souls didn't want to protect Island X. But leaving the *Hop* to guard a treasure on land wasn't exactly the kind of mission they were used to. They'd grown accustomed to life at sea, dressing up like ghouls in black cloaks and raiding the ships of pirates and King's Men. And they probably could have carried on like that forever (or at least until they were grown up) if Jem Fitzgerald and his uncle Finn hadn't gotten themselves kidnapped by pirates. The Lost Souls had staged a rescue, and it turned out that Jem was in possession of a map to the storied treasure everyone was looking for. (Although no one knew quite what it was.) When he got separated from Uncle Finn, he joined the Lost Souls in a hunt for both the treasure and his uncle. A few jungle treks, bouts of treason on board the *Hop*, and battles with bloodthirsty pirates later, here they were, the guardians of Island X and all its treasures.

Scarlet only wished the Lost Souls could share her enthusiasm for the new mission. Maybe if she taught them more about the island, she mused, they'd feel more connected to it. But then, that would require her to remember all the details she'd forgotten in the past seven years. And at the rate she was remembering these days, that would take a while. She sighed again. It was all rather complicated.

"But don't you worry," she said, turning back to the aras, not caring if they understood English or not. "We'll protect the treasure from anyone who dares trespass. And not just the rubies. We're here to protect *all* of Island X."

She knew the Islanders would have appreciated that; it was this special, untouched place they'd valued, not some shiny red rocks. If the treasure hunters were to discover Island X's riches, they'd take not only every jewel on it, but also every tree and animal they pleased— just as they had on all the other islands.

"Don't you worry," Scarlet repeated, sounding far braver than she felt. "We've got a plan." She began to climb back down the tree to call the crew together to make that plan.

Scarlet had barely set foot in the clearing when she ran into eleven-year-old Jem Fitzgerald and his uncle Finn, who was supposedly a famous botanist on the other side of the world. Scarlet still thought that Finnaeus Bliss, with his very bald head and sweaty, egg-shaped body, looked nothing like a famous person should. But then, from what she'd heard, things were a little backward in the Old World.

"It's really the *Bediotropicanus onicus* that we're after," Uncle Finn was telling Jem, who seemed to be trying hard to stay awake. Uncle Finn tended to go on at length about plants. "It's one of the most riveting *Bedio*s I've heard of, and that's saying something! The structure of its anthers, you see—"

Scarlet decided that this was a fine time to interject and stepped toward them. "Are you off then, Uncle Finn?" He wasn't *her* uncle, of course, but all the Lost Souls had taken to calling him "Uncle Finn." They might never have admitted to missing their own parents, whom they'd either abandoned to join the Lost Souls or who'd abandoned them, but they were happy to take on a surrogate uncle.

Jem looked relieved at the interruption. Uncle Finn mopped his forehead with his handkerchief. "I am, indeed, Captain. Off on the trail of a plant that could change our lives."

Scarlet studied the sweaty scientist. Uncle Finn could be a little dramatic when it came to plants, but this sounded interesting. "Really? What is it?"

"A bromeliad."

"Oh." Scarlet herself wouldn't have known a bromeliad to see one, but she knew better than to admit that to Uncle Finn.

"A bromeliad that will"—he paused for effect—"cure the world of androgenetic alopecia."

Scarlet's eyes widened. "Really?"

Jem raised an eyebrow at her. "Do you know what that is?"

She shook her head. "Not a clue. But it sounds terrible."

"It is," Uncle Finn said solemnly.

"It's baldness," Jem said, blowing a lock of hair out of his eyes. "Hair loss."

"Oh." Scarlet looked from Jem to his uncle. "A bromeliad can cure that?"

Uncle Finn nodded. "I believe so. It'll take some

searching, though. And some intense experimentation. Fortunately, I've acquired a research assistant," he said, just as a monstrous man in tattered trousers came running toward them.

"Finn! Finn, I'm ready!" the man shouted. A cutlass hanging from his belt slapped his tree-trunk leg as he ran.

"Thomas?" Scarlet looked at Jem, who grinned.

The giant Thomas skidded to a stop in front of them, gasping for breath. "Thought . . . thought ye'd left without me. I was worried there."

Uncle Finn reached up to pat Thomas's shoulder. "I wouldn't leave without you, Thomas. I was just saying a few words to Jem before we go."

"Right. Course. I was . . . I was just worried."

Scarlet, Jem, and Uncle Finn all smiled at him. It was hard to believe that just a month ago Thomas had actually helped the treasure-hungry pirates kidnap Jem and Uncle Finn. It hadn't been his idea, of course—he'd worked on the *Dark Ranger*, a pirate ship captained by a nasty, rodentlike man with a very long name that Scarlet could never remember. But Thomas had proven himself a hero twice: first when he'd smuggled Uncle Finn off the ship and later when Captain What's-his-name had gotten his hands on the treasure map and intercepted the Lost Souls and Uncle Finn on Island X. There, beside the island's steamy Boiling Lake, Thomas had denied his captain's orders to do away with the children and taken their side instead.

Scarlet sighed happily at the memory. Thomas was a jolly pirate. She'd miss him while he was off on this new adventure, but she could tell he was happy as a clam to be a real research assistant.

"Now, Jem, Scarlet." Uncle Finn stuffed his handkerchief in his pocket. "We'll be gone a few days. And I wouldn't be a good uncle if I didn't say this."

"Uncle Finn, we—" Jem began to protest.

"Quiet, boy. We've seen many dangers on this island—"

"But—" Scarlet interjected, ready to assure him that she was well aware of all the dangers. Uncle Finn stopped her with a wave of his hand.

"*But* we've been here a month, and all seems well. Plus, I know the Lost Souls are capable of taking care of themselves. Lord knows if you can sail a ship and raid schooners without getting caught, you can camp alone on an island. *However*, you mustn't forget the dangers. Yes, the animals might be on your side. Yes, the spirits seem to be looking out for you. But the Dread Pirate Captain Wallace Hammerstein-Jones—"

"*That's* his name!" Scarlet exclaimed, and received a glare from Uncle Finn. "Sorry. I just . . . it's a long name," she murmured.

Finn cleared his throat. "You mustn't forget about Captain Wallace. He has our old map, and he'll be back. So promise me you'll be careful."

Scarlet and Jem mumbled their promises.

"Good. And if you need me, I won't be far away. In fact . . ." He reached into his pocket and pulled out a funny little pipe about the size of Scarlet's pinkie finger. "I'll leave this with you. It looks harmless, but believe me, it will shatter the nearest eardrum. If you need me"—he tossed Jem the pipe—"just call."

"All right." Jem tucked it in his pocket.

"Well then. Thomas, if you're ready."

Thomas straightened and saluted. "At yer service, Cap'n Finn."

Uncle Finn shook his head. "Just Finn, Thomas. We're off then. Take care, you two."

"We will," Scarlet and Jem chorused. They followed the researchers to the edge of the clearing, then stood and waved until they disappeared behind the curtain of leaves and vines.